TIME
LOCK

TIME LOCK

A NOVEL

HOWARD BERK
AND
PETER BERK

IE Snaps
by
IngramElliott

TimeLock

Published by IngramElliott, Inc.
www.ingramelliott.com
9815-J Sam Furr Road, Suite 271, Huntersville NC 28078

This is a work of fiction. The names, characters, places, or events used in this book are the product of the author's imagination or used fictitiously. Any resemblance to actual people (alive or deceased) events, or locales is completely coincidental.

Book formatting by Creative Publishing Book Design
Cover design by: H.O. Charles
Editing by: Angela Glennon
Editing by: Katherine Bartis

ISBN Paperback: 978-1-952961-07-6
ISBN E-Book: 978-1-952961-08-3

Library of Congress Control Number: 2022939155

Subjects: Fiction—Action and Adventure. Fiction—Thrillers—Suspense.

Published in the United States of America. Printed in the United States of America.

First Edition: 2022, First International Edition: 2022

The *TimeLock* series by
Howard Berk and Peter Berk

TimeLock

A sci-fi-tinged action-adventure with heart and humor, *TimeLock* is the first in a new series of novellas set in the crime-ridden near future where a bold new technology transforms the justice system and challenges America's moral compass. Only one problem—what happens if you're innocent?

Coming Soon

TimeLock 2

Morgan Eberly's exciting adventures continue in a race around the globe fraught with danger and a frightening evolution of TimeLock technology.

Howard and Peter circa 1990

Dedication

For my beloved father, Howard, without whom this book – or this life – wouldn't have been possible.

ACKNOWLEDGMENTS

My deepest gratitude to the entire IngramElliott team for their warmth, support, guidance, and wisdom. I'll be forever grateful for their belief in these novels and hope to enjoy a long and rewarding association with them for many, many years to come.

PROLOGUE

"**E**berly!"

Oh God. This is it.

My name bounces off the cold gray walls of the stark waiting room. It's still hard to believe this incredibly futuristic complex is surrounded by a dilapidated century-old prison. But it's even harder to believe that this very same futuristic complex is about to steal forty years of my life in a matter of minutes.

Sitting on a shaky old folding chair, I put my head in my hands in the absurd hope that the two guards near the control room entrance won't see me and will simply move on to the next inmate.

Yeah, right.

Seconds later, both guards head my way. If I resist, they'll just subdue me. If I run, they'll just catch me. If I scream, they'll just ignore me.

1

With my knees shaking and my heart pounding, I slowly rise—resigned, terrified, and utterly defeated.

The glassed-off control room is a bright oasis of light. Capsules with transparent canopies continuously depart the room for the processing chamber. Pipes high up on the wall start hissing out a fine spray of gas that's funneled directly into each capsule.

Once I've climbed inside my own capsule, the canopy closes with a faint hum. At first, I don't feel a thing—other than abject terror, of course. It's almost relaxing. Maybe they should turn this place into a day spa. A bright blue glow engulfs the interior of the capsule and then a dazzling kaleidoscope of multicolored lights fills the tiny space around me. An oddly scented spray starts blanketing me from head to toe.

Somehow, I'm both shivering from cold and burning from heat as if trapped in an otherworldly fusion of ice storm and fiery inferno.

But it might just be the incredibly loud, incredibly deep rumbling hum that's the most terrifying assault of all. I try to move, but there's nowhere to go.

Please, someone, help me.

CHAPTER ONE

TWO MONTHS EARLIER

For the time being, I'm twenty-three. At six foot one, I'm fairly athletically built with dark wavy hair and what I've been told is an especially ingratiating smile I should showcase more often.

My name is Morgan Eberly, and I'm bored out of my mind. The thing is, I've always had a problem staying focused—school, relationships, work. Apparently, I was born with a mild ADD condition, but the real issue for me—and forgive the immodesty—is that I'm really, really smart. As in always a beat or two ahead of my classmates growing up and already a college graduate (computer science, Maryland Tech) at eighteen.

If only my dad had been around to see it. Far brighter than I'll ever be, he, too, was a tech whiz and, in fact, helped design a supercomputer a decade ago that remains the industry's gold standard to this day. Unfortunately, his brilliance made him a highly sought-after consultant around the world, and it was on one of his frequent trips to China that he was killed in a train derailment seven years ago.

My mom is still around, thank God, but she's never really recovered from the loss. She's only forty-five, but after my father died, she seemed to age twenty years overnight, much as I soon will. I guess it runs in the family.

As is my daily custom here in the land of nonstop excitement, I'm sitting in my cubicle, watching the clock and wondering yet again why I took such a banal job at QuickRight Financial Services.com. I could tell you what I do, but you'd probably nod off before I finished the sentence.

Here's the thing: I guess I'm toiling away at this snorefest of a job for my mother's sake. Not just for the money I give her every month, but because she deserves to know where I am and what I'm doing at least eight hours a day. This after seven sleepless years spent watching her only child drift in and out of school, not to mention in and out of trouble, which all culminated in my arrest a year and a half ago for committing the wholly unoriginal but deeply satisfying act of punching out a guy in a bar.

Now, in my defense, the guy had it coming. My fellow motorcycle-loving pal Lonny Myers had just beaten this particular mouth breather out of fifty bucks in pool, and the man went flippo on him. Lonny, being rail thin and defenseless, didn't stand a chance. So, I stepped in and did my hero bit. The man and I went a few rounds, someone called the cops, and now I have a permanent record that seemed earth-shattering at the time, but will seem laughably innocuous a short twenty-four hours from now.

Unfortunately, nothing as exciting as a bar fight ever happens at QFS. Instead, like clockwork, two of my fellow programmers are headed my way for lunch, oblivious to the fact that, some days, I'd rather savor my pathetic little sandwich and chips alone.

Ben Varley is my age, very thin, and stands over six feet, five inches tall. Eric Fowler, by contrast, is Ben's polar opposite physically—short, chunky, and the proud-though-he-shouldn't-be owner of perhaps the scraggliest beard to be grown since Cro-Magnons roamed the Earth.

Despite my loner tendencies and occasional grumpiness, I like hanging out with these guys, usually at the dumpy apartment they share a couple of miles from here.

Losing my dad at a young age, I never had the chance to just be a kid, and they have a knack for bringing out my inner adolescent—the goofier, nerdier, more childlike side of myself that gets lost in the shadows whenever I'm pretending to be more mature and confident than I really am.

"Hey, guys," I mumble.

"Guess who our illustrious leader brought to tears yesterday?" Eric says with disgust.

I let out a sigh. Nolan Keeler. Pompous, egomaniacal, sexist. A man who doesn't deserve to be a regular employee, let alone our boss.

"Sara in accounting," Ben chimes in. "Sweetest girl ever. He throws this report on her desk and chews her out for ten minutes before it hits him it wasn't her report."

Eric nods his head and looks over at me, apparently trying to rally me to the cause. "But does the creep apologize?" he says. "No way. So, we were thinking . . ."

Here we go. I'm finally an adult, and these guys want to drag me back to grade school.

"Not again, boys," I say. "It was funny once . . ."

"So it'll be funny again," Ben says, a conspiratorial smile on his face. "Please, Morgan, you're the only one who can work him over."

Eric gives me one of his patented puppy dog faces, and then adds the capper: "For Sara?"

I give them my best stern face, but they know I'm crumbling fast. And then I cave completely. "Fine. But this is the last time." Sure it is.

Ben and Eric high five, then Ben says excitedly, "He's on his way in now! Better hurry!"

I throw a final scathing glance their way, but the reality is, I share their feelings. Not just about Sara, who I barely know, but about Keeler. If anyone deserves what I'm about to do, it's this clown, whose reign of terror seems to bring at least one employee to tears every day.

I hit the keyboard, and the boys huddle around. These guys are programming nerds like me, but even they can't help but be impressed with my virtuoso-like speed and dexterity.

And, seconds later, we're all staring at the monitor, on which a German luxury car site comes up. My fingers race around the keyboard like I'm a concert pianist on meth as the image switches to a page labeled Vehicle Security. I type in some more data, including a license plate number and driver's license info, and the page switches to a specific car: a brand-new coupe belonging to one Nolan Keeler.

I type in a few additional commands, and we start laughing because, even though we can't see inside his car, we know exactly what's going on at this very instant. The fat fuck is almost certainly listening to one of his pretentious opera channels, but the music is about to be superseded by a female navigation voice I've programmed in, which we can now hear shouting, "Turn left!"

A moment later, I direct Keeler's nav system to shout a new command: "Turn right!" The guys and I are starting to crack up, imagining what the incredulous Keeler must be doing right now. Then the nav voice screams, "Slow down, then back up. Stop dawdling!"

Now comes my favorite part. I hit a few keys, and the voice is not only louder than before but yelling at the no-doubt befuddled Keeler entirely in German: *"An der Kreuzung rechts!"* (Right at the intersection!), followed by *"Du fährst ja wie ein verrückter!"* (You're driving like a maniac!), and then finally, *"Sie werden den Behörden gemeldet!"* (You will be reported to the authorities!).

The three of us are howling with laughter like pre-pubescent idiots. But we're not done yet because—as expected—we now see Keeler's car just down the road and can make out the man himself inside frantically trying to get rid of his uninvited new German passenger. And it just keeps getting better.

"Oh God!" shouts Ben. "He's going through the car wash!"

Adds Eric, "Morgan—you've got to do it!"

I'm in all the way now, so I nod and say in feigned resignation, "A guy's gotta do what a guy's gotta do."

We look out the window as Keeler's car approaches the drive-through car wash two buildings away. Keeler runs his credit card through and drives forward. I tap into his car's rear camera, and we can tell when it's stopped and is undergoing the wash cycle. Seconds later, the car is being drenched in soap and water—and that's my cue.

I hit a few keys and program the car to lower all its windows. *If only he were driving a convertible,* I think.

We can now picture the drenched Keeler desperately trying to raise the windows back up. At last, his car emerges, and a thoroughly soaked Keeler gets out, opens his trunk, and finds a towel. As he dries himself off, he watches haplessly as the windows of his possessed, bilingual car go back up. He screams what we assume is a colorful collection of curse words as the three of us high five.

So immature. And so satisfying.

Our laughter continues for a minute, then the moment is shattered by my cell phone. Jesus, it's my sometime friend Lonny Myers.

The very definition of a perennial loser, Lonny is actually a decent sort if you make it past his criminal tendencies, ragged appearance, and wannabe-tough-guy persona. Surprisingly smart, I often thought he might have made something of himself if a couple of unfortunate bad-parenting clichés hadn't gotten in his way: an absentee father and an alcoholic mother. But instead of rising above his troubled upbringing, Lonny turned to holding up liquor stores and minimarts, leading—to nobody's great surprise—to his arrest and conviction for armed robbery four months ago.

What did turn out to be a surprise was that the timing of Lonny's arrest qualified him under a just-passed

Maryland law to become one of the very first prisoners to be processed through the hugely controversial prison program everyone in the country continues to talk about—TimeLock.

I give Eric and Ben a "got to take this" gesture, and they move off.

"Lonny! Where've you been? You got out a month ago!"

"Morgan . . . something's wrong." I expected his voice to sound older. After all, the man got a ten-year sentence for his latest robbery. (It would have been at least twice that if he had been using a loaded weapon.) But he sounds as frail as an old man, not to mention terrified out of his mind.

"What's wrong?" I ask.

Lonny responds, "I don't know," his voice shaky.

"You know I tried to visit you before you . . . went through. And I've been looking all over the place for you since you got out."

"Sorry. I didn't want anyone to see me."

"Where are you?"

"Baylor Park."

"I'll be right there."

"No—not here, Morgan! I have to see you alone."

11

"All right. Remember my family's cabin, up at the lake? We rode up there last summer? Meet me there at eight o'clock. If I'm late, the key is in the red planter."

"Okay . . . but don't be late. *Please.*"

CHAPTER TWO

Although my dad made a good living, he probably could have earned a lot more than he did. But he really didn't care because he was the least materialistic person I ever knew. No fancy car. No expensive jewelry. Just one passion: the outdoors.

For me, the outdoors means a long, open road and a fully loaded motorcycle, but Jackson Eberly was a true outdoorsman—camping, hiking, fishing, climbing, the works. Which is why he built us a cabin in Thurmont, Maryland, ten years ago, where our little family could time travel back to the days before cell phones, televisions, and computers.

I loved him anyway.

It's almost eight o'clock in the evening, and I ride up on my brand-new Harley. (Please don't tell my mom—she only sees me in a fifteen-year-old Honda Accord.) I'm on a quiet two-lane road near a lake, the first time I've been up here in years. I've begged my mother to sell the place, but she seems to think it would dishonor Dad's memory. Or something.

I spot the cabin and am instantly flooded both with memories and with guilt. The truth is that I never shared my dad's love of nature. Much too slow and quiet for me.

Four times a year, we'd come up here, and, every single time, I couldn't wait to leave. God knows I wanted to please my father, and I really did my best not to complain, but my dad knew I was out of my element here. Constant stimulation was more my speed, and we both knew that however much I tried to be a doting little boy following his sheriff father to the fishing hole, country life most definitely wasn't my speed.

Seven years later, I would give anything for another quiet night with my dad just reading a book, playing a board game, staring into the fireplace, looking at the stars, or doing absolutely nothing but being together.

I park the bike and do one of my signature flashy dismounts, trying to impress the neighborhood deer, I

14

guess. I move toward the cabin door and notice a faint light emanating from within. The door is partially open, and I've seen enough movies to know this can't be a good thing.

As I move inside, I hear a voice on the back porch saying, "We're really sorry about this, Lonny."

To which a tremulous-sounding Lonny responds, "How do you know my name?"

As I run toward the porch, the same man says, "We know everything about you. We know when you were born, and we know when you're going to die."

Just as I reach the back door, I hear two gunshots. I look outside and see two men, one of whom is wearing an oversized metallic watchband that reflects the back porch light. Not spotting me, both men hurry off around the side of the cabin, and I rush to the crumpled Lonny. I can't be sure, but I swear he sees me tearfully leaning over him and clutching both his shoulders right before he succumbs to his wounds.

I let out a plaintive "No!" and pull out my cell phone, but there's no reception. And the landline inside the cabin was discontinued years ago. I cover Lonny with my jacket and realize I need to get to the police station—or at least closer to a cell phone tower—so I bolt out the front door. And that's when I hear a gun bark twice, bullets barely missing me. I race away from the cabin and head toward the woods, pulling out my cell again and desperately hoping I can get a signal. No chance. Welcome to the outdoors. I look back and see a tall, silhouetted figure bolting toward me.

As I race past thick foliage and jump a couple of gullies, I glance back again to see the second man joining the first, both now charging my way. Breathlessly, I climb a three-post fence, roll down an incline, and then scramble through rocks and boulders. I bet these guys are at least a decade older than I am, but they're obviously in great shape, and it's only a matter of time before they catch up with me.

But I do have one advantage. I've been here before. Many times. In fact, this is the path to the lake my dad and I used to take to go out fishing. Which is why I know of an old abandoned pier where I can hide until . . . Then it hits me—the footsteps behind me have gone silent. The two goons have either stopped dead in their tracks waiting for me to show myself, or they've given up.

I hear the sound of a car engine. Ever so tentatively, I make my way back up to the road just in time to spot a black sedan rocketing off. I squint, trying to make out the Maryland license plate, but I can only see the last three numbers. I type them into my phone. And it's only now that I become aware of a bright glow on the horizon.

I race toward the cabin, and it's engulfed in flames.

Two hours later, I'm still staring at the smoldering cabin, now reduced to a mass of fragmented beams and black ash. Fire trucks and police cars are everywhere. One of the cops I've been talking to scribbles some more notes and nods to his partner. I think they're finally done with me.

"We have your address and cell," the first cop says. "Don't go too far."

I've just witnessed a friend being shot dead, almost suffered the same fate myself, and then watched our family cabin burn to the ground, but I'm not getting any sympathy from the police. In fact, they're looking at me more like a suspect than a victim.

I climb on my bike and roar off.

CHAPTER THREE

'm used to being a little hyper, but I don't remember ever being this wired. Obviously, I'm still shaken up by what happened to Lonny and almost happened to me. Which is why I stayed at a buddy's house last night, too scared to go home and too worried about involving my mother to stay with her.

I tried to do a little digging, but the fact of the matter is, I don't think Lonny had any real friends other than his half brother Cole Vinton and me. And we were more biker buddies than close pals. The few guys who knew him all claim they lost touch with him after his conviction, and, for the moment, I have no reason to doubt them because the same thing happened to me.

Lonny didn't want people to see him scared, I guess, and being one of the very first guinea pigs to be processed through that abomination of justice called TimeLock no doubt terrified him to his core.

For now, I have to assume that Lonny went back to his old ways once he got out—a bitter irony considering Governor Myra Winters's promise that her "revolutionary" program would scare criminals straight for life. Maybe he was dealing, though that was never his thing. Clearly, though, he teed off the wrong people, they followed him to the cabin, killed him, then tried to eliminate the only witness: me. It tracks, but only to a point. Why burn down the whole cabin?

That's why, after stopping to see Lonny's half brother and then my mom, I'm going to the police station to demand answers to a few rather important questions, such as who killed Lonny, who tried to kill me, and what in God's name this is all about.

Lonny talked tough but looked fragile. His maternal half brother Cole, on the other hand, talks tough and looks even tougher. Tall, burly, and decidedly unfriendly, he's about the last person I want to be with right now, excepting my would-be assassins, of course. But maybe, just maybe, he knows who's responsible for Lonny's murder.

After Cole lets me into his dingy apartment, I tell him about Lonny's murder. Although he and Lonny weren't close, I expect a bit more of a reaction than the shrug I get and the words that follow.

"I always figured he wouldn't make it to twenty-five," Cole says unemotionally. If I were twice as brave and five times as big, I'd punch this heartless guy in the face for being so indifferent to the murder of his only sibling. But all that would get me is a broken nose, so I remind myself I'm not here to make a condolence call—I'm here to get some answers.

But the answers may have to wait for a few more minutes. Cole receives a work call and tells me to wait in the living room. With nothing else to do and no interest in the stack of trucking and gun magazines on the coffee table, I pick up the remote and turn on the television. After checking out a couple of channels, I finally settle on a cable news show called *Your Day* and find myself instantly transfixed because the two men on the screen are shouting about the very prison program Lonny recently went through—TimeLock.

"This isn't law and order," host Brian West is saying vociferously to his guest, Senator Harold Whelan of Texas. "This is madness. Your own president knew it but let Maryland Governor Myra Winters steamroll him into approving the trial program anyway!"

"Your party sure loves trotting out that one hot mic video, doesn't it? Sure, Governor Winters is passionate about TimeLock, and sure, President Bartlett needed to consider all sides of the equation before authorizing—"

"Please, Senator. The man looked as frightened as Oliver Twist asking for more. In fact, let's roll the tape now, and then you can tell us how we didn't see what we just saw."

I watch in bemusement as Senator Whelan strains futilely to hold back his discomfort at watching the famous video starring President William Bartlett and Governor Myra Winters. If I remember correctly, it was unintentionally filmed during an arts endowment fundraising party in DC back in 2030, and there's no question that, despite being in the presence of the supposed most powerful man in the world, Myra Winters is clearly running the show.

"I trust your family is well," says a seemingly uncomfortable President Bartlett, then fifty-nine. But utterly uninterested in small talk, the slightly younger—and still very attractive—Myra Winters breaks into a broad smile.

"They did it, Bill! It works!"

The president looks like he isn't sure whether to be jubilant or terrified.

"This is your moment, Mr. President. This is your chance to pull us back from the brink."

"You're asking me to unleash Frankenstein's monster," President Bartlett says.

"No, Mr. President. I'm asking you to approve a pilot program in one state—my state—that could bring crime to its knees."

"Do you begin to fathom how divisive this will be?" the president asks meekly.

Governor Winters puts her hands on his shoulders and stares into his eyes. What follows over the next minute or so will not only secure President Bartlett's reputation as a political milquetoast, but thrust Myra Winters into the national limelight as his most likely successor.

"So what? Let them march in the streets. Let them scream on the Sunday morning talk shows. What do you care? You man up, take a few hits, and you're out of here in two years. Then it's somebody else's problem."

Although the president apparently wants to be annoyed at her irreverence, he can't help but smile, no doubt thinking what I was thinking the first time I saw this: The woman has balls. Then the governor says: "Mr. President, may I speak frankly?"

President Bartlett shows a rare bit of wit with this comedic retort: "You mean up till now you've been holding back?"

Oblivious to his sarcasm, the governor says, "Sure, you can let the status quo continue. Dire economy. Desperate people turning to crime. An insanely overcrowded prison system that belongs in some impoverished third-world country and not in the United States of America. Or you can be the president who made the tough choice, who said, 'Enough! This country's downward spiral ends on my watch.' Mr. President, do this. Don't wimp out. Make history. Give me TimeLock!"

The image freezes with William Bartlett looking like a deer in the headlights—not just the headlights of a car, but the headlights of a ten-ton runaway train.

Much to Senator Whelan's relief, the video ends.

"I'll give him credit," West says. "The president knew it was insanity. If only he hadn't caved in."

"No, Brian, insanity is remaining idle when crime is turning our nation into a war zone. TimeLock is the ultimate deterrent. We're seeing that already. In states that have yet to approve the program, going to jail is often seen as a reward rather than a punishment. Food on the table and a roof over your head. Better than going hungry and homeless, wouldn't you say? But look at what's happening in Maryland and elsewhere. Criminals will do anything to avoid being processed through TimeLock because the punishment is so severe and so permanent. That's why the program works. And mark my words, it will be the law of the land whether you like it or not."

"You're probably right. It will be the law of the land one day. And I'll speak out against it as long as I have this platform because it's technology gone amok, and I've read enough history, seen enough news, and watched enough movies to know how that works out. My next guest is . . ."

Cole comes back in the room, and I shut off the TV.

"Hope you don't mind," I say. "Since Lonny went through, I'm following everything to do with TimeLock."

"If you ask me, I'm all for it. If Lonny had lived, I doubt he would have pulled another holdup job again in his life."

I didn't ask him, and I really don't care what he thinks. But I do care about what he knows.

25

"Listen, Cole," I say, "these guys meant business. They killed Lonny, they came after me, and, for reasons I still can't figure out, they burned down my family's cabin. So, I need to ask: Do you have any idea who might have done this or why?"

"Not a clue, man. Sorry."

"When was the last time you saw or spoke to Lonny?"

"Three, maybe four months ago. We didn't have much to talk about other than how our mother screwed up both our lives."

"I know he was into low-level robberies," I say, "which God knows I tried to talk him out of a hundred times. But what if he was involved with something bigger that he didn't let me in on? Like working with a loan shark or a drug dealer? Maybe he stole from them, and this was payback. I'm just guessing, of course, but does any of this ring a bell to you?"

"Not really. Lonny was small-time all the way. But if he got himself in deep shit like that, I'd be the last one he'd ever discuss it with. I tried to get him to quit the stupid holdups too. Even offered him a job at the tire store where I work, but there was no reasoning with him. Eventually, we stopped talking about his private life, and then we stopped talking altogether. So, like I said, I'd be the last one to know what he was getting himself into."

"Okay, thanks anyway. I had to try."

"What did you say your name was again?"

"Morgan. Morgan Eberly."

Cole's hardened expression softens for a moment, and he says, "Let me know, will you, Morgan? We were close once, me and Lonny. Deep down, he was a good kid, and he deserved better."

"I couldn't agree more," I say, a wave of guilt washing over me for the hundredth time as I realize Lonny might still be alive if I hadn't suggested meeting him at a remote cabin at night—the perfect setting for a secluded, witness-free murder.

Outside, I'm about to climb onto my motorcycle when I spot a black sedan parked down the street. It's too far away to see the plates clearly, and I'm not even sure it's the same make as the one I saw last night, but an icy chill courses through me.

One thing's for sure, though—I'm not about to walk toward the car in case someone's inside waiting for me, so I start up my bike. But, before I take off, I notice Cole peering out his apartment window at me. If this is the sedan I saw at the cabin, is it possible that it belongs to *him*? Doesn't quite make sense—if he were involved in Lonny's murder, he wouldn't have let me walk out of his apartment, right? Then again, it seems like nothing in my life has made sense since last night, so all I can do is speed off and pray nobody follows me.

CHAPTER FOUR

I've put this off long enough—it's showtime. Time to put on the performance of a lifetime for one Grace Sharon Eberly, also known as my mother. If I haven't told her I still ride a motorcycle, I sure don't want to tell her about last night. But the cabin's in her name, so she'll find out soon enough. Better it come from me than the cops or some random insurance agent.

I park my car in front of my mom's modest home and head toward the door. As I do, I spot a black sedan rolling by, then it parks just ahead of me. I'm too far away from my car to get back in, so I start running as two guys get out of the sedan and rush toward me.

I duck down an alley, then emerge on another residential street. I look back, but the two men have mysteriously vanished. It feels like last night all over again. What could have made them stop in midpursuit, I wonder? Then I get my answer. Police and suits suddenly appear: five guys and one woman. I'm about to thank them for saving my life, so I'm beyond shocked when the woman points her gun at me and says, "Do not move precipitously, or you may be shot."

I kneel, and she gruffly pulls my arms behind my back and handcuffs me.

"What are you doing? Those guys tried to kill me!"

"Janine Price, FBI. You're under arrest for the murder of Lawrence Myers."

They read me my rights, and I'm taken away. The nightmare that is my soon-to-be-abbreviated life is just beginning.

CHAPTER FIVE

TWO MONTHS LATER

How can this be happening? My mother works as a secretary at a law firm, and one of the partners was kind enough to basically defend me pro bono. The guy is good—very good—but even he couldn't persuade the jury of my innocence.

The prosecution has a record of my phone call with Lonny before he was killed, they have a "witness" swearing she saw me roughhouse Lonny into the cabin. They have my fingerprints on what's left of Lonny's clothes after the fire. They have nothing on a black sedan or the two guys who chased me. And, just to

31

seal the deal, they have my conviction for assault from the bar incident.

My life is screwed, but it's my mother I'm most heartsick about. After my conviction a year and a half ago for that stupid bar fight, and before my arrest for Lonny's murder, we had finally been able to enjoy a few stable months free of torment and loss. She was starting to embrace life again, I had a steady job, and the loss of my dad had become more of a dull ache than an open wound.

"The defendant will rise," the judge says after my guilty verdict has been read. My mother, a dozen or so strangers, and FBI agent Janine Price look on. Off to the side is an expressionless Cole Vinton.

"Morgan Jordan Eberly, you have been found guilty of second-degree murder. Accordingly, I hereby sentence you to forty years imprisonment."

My head drops, and I can't bear to look my mother's way. Agent Price seems neither pleased nor disappointed; my fate means nothing to her personally. She's done her job.

A few days later, I'm taken in a police car to my new domicile: Loomis Detention Center. The same home away from home where Lonny spent most of his final days. Which means I'm in line to be processed just like he was.

As we approach the prison complex, at least a hundred protesters are outside marching up and down the street. Most are carrying signs, including "Stop the Insanity: End TimeLock Now!" and "Don't Fool with Mother Nature!" Several TV vans are parked nearby, and at least a dozen cameras and newscasters dot the scene along with about twenty-five other reporters and photographers. Sensing a money-making opportunity, a few vendors are even selling tasteless "collectibles," such as pro and con TimeLock T-shirts, caps, and mugs. One industrious merchant almost makes me smile with such prison-themed items as TimeLock-labeled handcuffs and even a fake cake with a large file sticking out of it.

My near-smile fades quickly, however, once I'm gruffly processed inside—handing over my belongings, taking off my clothes, and saying goodbye to my freedom.

Dressed in prison garb, I'm escorted to my cell, which is empty while my "bunkie" is enjoying his one-hour workout time in the yard.

Not that I'm a fan of the governor's wacko new program, but I do agree that something has to be done about prison overcrowding because, even with TimeLock underway, this place is the ultimate Room 101 for claustrophobics. Crime is rampant nationwide since the economic meltdown of 2028, and most every prison is packed like Times Square on New Year's Eve. Loomis may be one of the worst. No wonder Governor Winters chose this place for her experiments. If her projections are accurate, the number of criminals here will drop by half by the end of the year.

Considering what the program does to you—what it's about to do to me—I believe the projections.

On my third day here, I join a parade of inmates all being ushered into a small auditorium. Somehow, I have a feeling we're not here to see a revival of *The Music Man*. Among the other invited guests is my terrifying cellmate Kyle Bannon, an impossibly fit former Navy SEAL who was convicted for manslaughter after a hit-and-run in his pickup truck three months ago.

The room seats sixty or seventy, each one of us now reacting to the ominous booming sound of the doors being closed behind us. I'm seated next to a couple of guys I've managed to exchange a handful of syllables with since my arrival: Charlie Rajek, about forty and in for armed robbery, and Calvin Perry, a thirty-fiveish former pro linebacker who stupidly got caught up in drug trafficking. My bunkie, Kyle Bannon, takes a seat next to me and surprises me by uttering the longest sentence I've heard out of him since my arrival: "I didn't do it, man."

Given that I'm about to be processed for a crime *I* didn't commit, I find myself actually believing him.

Our collective mumbling and grumbling grinds to a quick halt when a number of men and one woman—Maryland Governor Myra Winters herself, unquestionably the chief proponent of TimeLock from its conception—enter the auditorium and briskly stomp onto the stage. Warden Leland Schaeffer detaches from the others and moves to the podium.

I'm half expecting an opening joke, but Schaeffer gets right to the point: "Under Maryland law, all of you are to be processed through an experimental program under the jurisdiction of the Bureau of Prisons, Department of Justice. On my left is Governor Myra Winters, who has helped guide this trial program through the legislature."

Playing his role of emcee to the hilt, Schaeffer actually pauses for a moment as if we're all about to break into applause after the illustrious governor's introduction.

"This is it, boys—TimeLock," Rajek says.

"I don't know," replies Perry. "Sounds pretty good to me. Over in a day, home in a few weeks."

"And what if you aren't guilty?" I offer, prompting Bannon to nod in agreement.

Perry smiles. "Well, then, you're shit out of luck, aren't you?"

My thoughts exactly.

On the stage, the warden continues serving as host of this fun-filled gathering. "At this time, I would also like to introduce Patrick Loder."

Loder is a commanding middle-aged man, impeccably dressed, and totally confident. Behind him, a large screen descends. The lights go down, and the screen is filled with the image of an ultramodern glass and steel building.

"My name is Patrick Loder, and I'm the CEO of a company called Genescence, which developed the technology behind TimeLock." Something tells me most of my fellow inmates don't realize that the name Genescence is a combination of the words "genetics" and "senescence" —the process of aging.

How clever. How terrifying.

The image on the screen behind Loder cuts to a high-tech lab. A number of white-coated figures can be seen in the background, with a distinguished-looking older man in the foreground.

Loder continues: "The man you see here is Dr. Lionel Garvey. He is a well-known geneticist, twice nominated for the Nobel Prize. I tell you this because, while his credentials may not normally be of interest to you, they may be of comfort as you prepare to pay your debt to society."

The image on the screen changes to a close-up shot of a young man in profile. Then a full-face shot.

"This man's name is Vincent Amici," says Loder. "He was sentenced for a series of armed robberies. Vincent's crime spree took him through five states and a dozen convenience stores. The grand total of his 'take' was $3,703."

Loder's tone makes all that effort for $3,703 sound as stupid as it is, and many of the prisoners laugh. I, however, am not feeling especially jovial at the moment. In fact, I'm getting more petrified by the second.

"Dumb," Loder says. "The only smart thing about Vincent was his choice of weapon: a water pistol. His sentence? Twelve years."

At this, the on-screen image changes, and we're looking at the same profile shot, followed by the same face shot from the front. But something's different. Something some of us don't realize at first.

"This is Vincent Amici after TimeLock. Now, for those of you who may have been too busy to follow the news recently, I'm sure you're curious what TimeLock is. Okay, let's take another look."

On the screen, the first profile and full face are slotted above the second profile and full face. Now, we can compare.

"The difference is twelve years," Loder continues, and you better believe there isn't a prisoner in this auditorium who isn't hanging on his every word now.

"In the photos on top, Vincent is twenty-seven years old. In the photos on the bottom, Vincent is thirty-nine."

Here, Loder pauses for dramatic effect and, as intended, the effect is dramatic indeed when he adds: "These pictures were taken the same day."

For the vast majority of us, this is hardly a revelation since we already know what this insane program does. But, among a few, there's an incredulous buzz.

Loder again: "Question: What happened to Vincent? Answer: He was processed through TimeLock."

The on-screen video now shows a younger Vincent Amici being escorted into a radiant-white room. He wears a silver metallic suit. He approaches a long black horizontal capsule laid out along a magnetic track. The canopy is open. With emotionless aplomb, Vincent clambers into the capsule. The canopy electronically closes. The capsule glides forward on the magnetic track. It looks like some nightmarish scene straight out of a sci-fi movie.

On the screen, attendants supervise dials, gauges, instrument panels, and various monitors. Loder continues his narration: "As the name implies, TimeLock's incredibly advanced technology locks in the exact duration of your sentence in years, days, and even hours before you undergo a genetic acceleration process that takes a mere seven minutes. Side effects have been minimal to nonexistent, and the procedure itself is painless and safe." Another dramatic pause. This guy's sadistic theatrics are really starting to annoy me.

"Mr. Amici?" Loder says.

With this, one member of the onstage group moves to join Loder. Not an actor, but the real Vincent Amici. There's more murmuring from the crowd as the prisoners recognize him. As if he's happy to be here, Amici waves cheerfully.

Now, it's Governor Winters's turn. She strides to the podium, every bit as commanding and self-assured as Loder.

"Following TimeLock processing," she begins, "a three-week observation period is required, followed by conventional parole procedures. Bottom line? The prisoner has served his time. He is free."

As if she and Loder graduated from the same method acting school, now it's the governor's turn to take a theatrical pause. After a beat, she continues: "Let me add a caution. TimeLock is a program of punishment, not a reward for criminals. It substitutes one kind of time for another. Instead of aging in a cell, the prisoner's body is aged. For now, male prisoners only, but in a few weeks, women as well. So, if you've committed an act of violence or have had three convictions in this state within the last year—even minor convictions—you will be processed through TimeLock. No exceptions. You will pay a price for your crimes, and that price will be a chunk of your life."

Rajek, Perry, Bannon, and I exchange glances—four tough guys desperately trying to pretend we're not all scared shitless. My God, who even needs a TimeLock capsule at this point? Just *hearing* what we're about to go through has already aged the four of us at least a decade.

CHAPTER SIX

It's the next day, and I'm at a table in the visitors' room. I rise as Janine Price walks in, once again wearing a well-cut suit. Businesslike but very feminine. She's at least five foot eight with longish dark hair and a surprisingly sweet smile that makes me almost forgive her for arresting me. In other words, she may have ruined my life, but Agent Price is quite attractive, even if she is, in her early thirties, a bit old for me. For now.

"I received your query. You have a question. What is it?"

Just the warm and fuzzy greeting I was expecting. Fine, we're not here for speed dating. I'll get right to the point too.

"Why did the FBI get involved in Lonny's death?" I ask.

"I know he's been a friend of sorts, but perhaps you don't know that 'friend Lonny' had been tied up with a counterfeiting ring out of Oakwood. We pulled in the gang that day. We were going to pull in Lonny too, but you had a different kind of justice in mind for him."

"I didn't kill him, damn it!" My shouting scores a harsh glance from the guard.

Janine responds, "All evidence to the contrary."

"And remind me again what my motive was to suddenly murder an old friend or set fire to my own family's cabin."

"Caught him robbing you? You wanted to burn the evidence of what you did?"

"I was there to help him. He was in some kind of trouble."

"A neighbor saw you pull a gun on him, force him inside."

"I don't own a gun, Ms. Price. And that neighbor was watching from fifty yards away at night. What she saw is the real killer, not me. By the way, did anyone check out Lonny's half brother, Cole?"

"The trial's over, Mr. Eberly. This conversation is moot."

"Sorry to trouble you with my life," I respond.

"Why am I here?"

"Pathetic as it is, you're all I've got."

"Then you've got nothing."

"Don't you get it? I need time to track Lonny's real killers down. I go through tomorrow, and my life's over."

Janine's tone grows a tiny bit softer. "Listen to me, Morgan, I'm no fan of TimeLock, but it's the law in this state, and there's nothing I can do about it."

I sense a small opening and ask, "Is it just you, or is the whole FBI against it?"

"You kidding? They love it. TimeLock is the greatest single deterrent against crime in this country's history."

"I believe it. Three strikes and you're old—very old."

Much to my surprise, Janine suddenly becomes positively chatty. Clearly, TimeLock has gotten under her skin. "You want my take? It's a monstrosity. It may work as a deterrent, but at what cost? All it does is get convicted criminals out on the cheap. Nothing learned except they put one over on society! What's the lesson TimeLock teaches? Not a damn thing except your punishment is a bargain basement slap on the wrist!"

"You're forgetting one other thing. Who gives you all those years back if it turns out you were innocent?"

That should melt her. But instead, she rises, our small connection once again severed. "Morgan, this is pointless. If you killed Lonny Myers, you're getting what you deserve. If you didn't, well then . . . life sucks."

She hesitates a second and produces a slight smile. "Go ahead and say it. Onetime free pass."

I manage a small smile of my own. "Bitch."

"Thank you," she says and heads for the exit.

CHAPTER SEVEN

It's our turn to be Vincent Amici. Later today, I'll be sixty-three. I hope the senior discount at the movie theatre will make it all worth it.

Charlie Rajek, Calvin Perry, Kyle Bannon, and I are among the three dozen or so seated in the waiting area inside the TimeLock complex at Loomis we saw in Loder's little home video. On our left is a gleaming high-tech control room, and in front of us is a vast processing facility replete with dozens of black see-through capsules gliding along a magnetic track into a separate processing area.

Dressed as we all are in silver-sheened coveralls, my fellow inmates and I look like the cast of some cheesy low-budget alien invasion film from the 1950s. My heart's pounding wildly, and, along with the ever-present fear and anger, I find myself consumed by sadness. The same kind of sadness patients must feel when told they only have a short time to live.

"So here we are at Camp Auschwitz. Right, gang?" Rajek says.

"You know what I heard?" Perry says. "Somebody fucked up yesterday, and three guys fried like eggs going through."

Perry half smiles at his pathetic attempt at gallows humor, then becomes wide-eyed when an attendant signals to him. As he slowly walks over to a capsule, he manages a glance back our way, i.e.: Hey! No big deal! But it doesn't come off.

Perry hesitates, and two guards approach. He tries to fight them off, but it's no use. Finally, he climbs into the capsule and slides down to a reclining position. The canopy slowly closes. The capsule moves off, Perry's screams eerily distant.

"Eberly!"

Oh God. This is it.

My name bounces off the cold gray walls of the stark waiting room. It's still hard to believe this incredibly futuristic complex is surrounded by a dilapidated century-old prison. But it's even harder to believe that this very same futuristic complex is about to steal forty years of my life in a matter of minutes.

Sitting on a shaky old folding chair, I put my head in my hands in the absurd hope that the two guards near the control room entrance won't see me and will simply move on to the next inmate.

Yeah, right.

Seconds later, both head my way. If I resist, they'll just subdue me. If I run, they'll just catch me. If I scream, they'll just ignore me.

With my knees shaking and my heart pounding, I slowly rise—resigned, terrified, and utterly hopeless.

The glassed-off control room is a bright oasis of light. Capsules with transparent canopies continuously depart the room for the processing chamber. Pipes high up on the wall start hissing out a fine spray of gas that's funneled directly into each capsule.

Once I've climbed inside my own capsule, the canopy closes with a faint hum. At first, I don't feel a thing—other than abject terror, of course. It's almost relaxing. Maybe they should turn this place into a day spa. A bright blue glow engulfs the interior of the capsule and then a dazzling kaleidoscope of multicolored lights fills the tiny space around me. An oddly scented spray starts blanketing me from head to toe.

Somehow, I'm both shivering from cold and burning from heat as if trapped in an otherworldly fusion of ice storm and fiery inferno.

But it might just be the incredibly loud, incredibly deep rumbling hum that's the most terrifying assault of all. I try to move, but there's nowhere to go.

I can now see the processing room I'm gliding through, and I zero in on several large monitors covering a wall. Clearly, each monitor corresponds to a prisoner within his capsule. I can't see myself up there, but I do see Calvin Perry, and, through the haze, I think I can see the gradual change taking place as he's being aged. The nightmare is real, and I'm next.

Please, someone, help me.

CHAPTER EIGHT

Did seven minutes pass already? I guess I'm done, and I guess I'm old. But why has the capsule stopped moving?

Something's very wrong here, so I push the capsule open—no easy task for someone as physically weak and mentally drained as I am right this moment. I climb out, expecting a bunch of gruff guards to push me back in, but there's no one there. No one except a handful of other prisoners—Charlie Rajek and Calvin Perry among them—likewise climbing out of their capsules.

I make my way to an exit, and four or five other guys try to follow suit, but they're all quickly rounded up at gunpoint by at least ten just-arrived guards.

I move into a lobby area and spot 150 or so protesters who've just stormed the facility and apparently forced the temporary shutdown of TimeLock operations. The protesters are surrounded by a slew of guards trying to restore order. I realize I've just been given my one and only hope for escape. I find a storage room, take off my silver space suit, and throw on a ridiculously oversized janitorial outfit. I emerge back into the lobby area and ask one of the protesters to lend me his picket sign. As we're herded outside, I blend into the crowd, just another civilian—on a break from his job as a poorly dressed janitor, apparently—raging against the injustice of TimeLock.

Once we're escorted away from Loomis, I hand my picket sign to a woman and scurry off. Well, amble off is more like it—my knees hurt, and I feel ten pounds heavier. Then I remember I'm not twenty-three anymore. But what am I?

I'll have to worry about that new reality later. For now, it's time to get as far away from Loomis as possible. Sirens are blaring, and guards are running—some my way, others down another street. Fighting all instincts to run as far and as fast as possible, I instead move at a leisurely pace in an effort to continue blending in. I'm not dressed like a prisoner, so my best move is to hide in plain sight and not draw attention to myself.

I spot Charlie Rajek moving toward me. He's aged about fifteen years from what I can tell. Like me, he's managed to grab a disguise of sorts—in his case, a parka and wool cap. He sidles up next to me, and we both maintain a relaxed walking pace as we head away from Loomis toward an industrial area dotted with utility buildings and manufacturing plants.

"You look like shit, Eberly," Rajek says matter-of-factly.

"How many years?" I ask nervously.

"Fifteen? Twenty? About the same for me."

"I saw Perry running off. How'd he make out?"

"No idea. I feel weak and dizzy—how about you?"

"The same," I say. "It's all so weird. Like waking from a coma after two decades. I don't feel like me anymore."

"You're not you anymore. They've fucked us over big time. And it's gotta be worse for you. I was middle-aged when I went in, now I'm just more middle-aged. But you were a kid, and now . . ."

The last thing I want to do is let this tough guy see me cry, but I'm not sure I'll be able to hold it back. Yes, I managed to escape before the full forty-year sentence could be carried out, but I've still lost fifteen or more years of my life for a crime I didn't commit.

Rajek and I spot two police cars roaring past us on the way to Loomis, and fear overtakes sadness. Once the cars have passed, Rajek gestures, and we move behind a building. One thing is beyond obvious—we can't get caught now because they'd not only finish our TimeLock processing but add more years for escaping.

"Listen," Rajek says. "We can't be seen together. I have a brother-in-law who can take me in at Blue Lakes Resort. I used to be a short-order cook there. Where are you going to go?"

"I don't know. My mother lives an hour from here, but I can't put her through that. Plus, it's probably the first place they'll look. Maybe my friends from work."

"It's not right," Rajek says contemplatively. "What they did to us isn't right. TimeLock is more of a crime than anything I ever did."

"You got that right," I say. "Take care, Charlie."

"You too, man. Don't let them catch you, or you're done for."

I nod, and he moves off. Where I'm headed now—today and for the rest of my life—I haven't got a clue.

CHAPTER NINE

An hour and a half later, I'm staring into the mirror inside a run-down gas station bathroom. It's impossible to take in. Rajek was right, I must be twenty years older: salt and pepper hair, wrinkles around the eyes, the vestiges of my baby face long gone. Not for the first time, I shake my head at the sight of myself. How time flies.

An hour or so after that, I make my way to Lonny's place to "borrow" one of his motorcycles and a change of clothes. Obviously, I don't dare go to my apartment or my mom's house. I've got to let her know I'm okay, but any direct contact will bring the cops down on me within minutes.

What I should do, of course, is run for the hills, change my name, and never be seen again. But I can't do that to my mother—plus there's the small matter of looking over my shoulder the rest of my life. I have a few friends, including my guys at QFS and a couple of ex-girlfriends who would probably help me, but for now, I can't mix them up in this.

No, there's really only one way out of this nightmare: finding out who really killed Lonny and why.

I ride up to Curtis Bay Bar & Grill, a frequent haunt. The place I met Lonny, actually. Nearby, a couple of guys my age—well, not anymore, obviously—are fussing over their bikes. Reflexively, I try my famous athletic swirl dismount, forgetting I've aged twenty years since the last time I tried it. I promptly go tumbling to the ground. The two guys look on, and I'm sure they're about to laugh at this middle-aged loser trying to look young and cool.

But instead of laughing, they do something far more humiliating—they help me up. I've been in denial since Loomis, but it finally sinks in: I'm not a kid anymore.

"Thanks," I say to the guys. This morning, I was their peer; tonight, I could be their father.

Recovering as much poise as I can, I head into the bar. Fortunately, Lonny had some cash lying around, and I had no choice but to take it. First to buy a few disposable prepaid phones, and, right now, to buy a few desperately needed beers.

I also took another risk this afternoon, but it's worth it. I sent Ben at QFS an encrypted message I don't think even the FBI could crack. In the message, I asked him to surreptitiously let my mom know I'm okay, that I got something of a stay by the governor and my forty-year TimeLock sentence was cut in half. As far as she'll know, at least for now, I'm in a recovery center and doing fine, but not allowed to contact anyone for the next couple of weeks. Not sure she'll buy any of it, especially if my escape makes tonight's evening news or if the cops come knocking at her door looking for me, but it'll have to do for now.

I take a stool at the bar and am happy to see a familiar face approach. I hope he won't turn me in when he realizes who I am.

"Hey, Greg," I say.

"What can I get you, sir?"

"The usual," I respond. But Greg doesn't have a clue. "Heineken. Hang on, I've got my ID here somewhere."

Instinctively, I reach for my wallet before realizing it's in storage back at Loomis. But it doesn't matter. Greg gestures to indicate I shouldn't bother, and produces a smirk that shouts, "Does this aging clown actually think he might be *carded*?"

"That's okay, pal. I'll let it slide this time," he says.

He pours a beer, and once more I try to process the seismic shift in my life. But I'm not really here for beer or self-pity. I'm here for answers.

"Listen, Greg. You remember Lonny, right? Lonny Myers."

"Yeah, he was murdered."

"Do you know anyone who might have been after him?"

"How about the guy who killed him? A so-called friend he used to hang out with here. Hope he fries for what he did."

He just about did, I want to say. "Turns out it was the wrong guy."

"Who are you?" Greg asks.

"Please try to remember. A tall man, maybe works with a partner? Drives a black sedan?"

"No," a suddenly icy Greg says. "And this conversation is over."

I spot two cops entering the bar. I crouch down, praying they aren't looking for me. The cops take a seat, and I feign nonchalance as I move toward the door. Coming here was big-time dumb, I know. But what I'm about to do is far, far dumber.

CHAPTER TEN

Her line is ringing. Pick up, damn it! Come on—answer!

"Hello?" Agent Price says.

"I'm tossing the phone after this call, so don't bother tracing it."

"Not too smart running off like that, Morgan. Clever, but not smart. You know it's only a matter of time until we find you."

If she only knew I was walking on a beach not ten miles from her FBI office.

"At least this way I *have* time," I say. "Back at the cabin, when Lonny's killers took off? I saw Maryland plates but could only make out the last three numbers— five, four, seven."

"Did you give them to the police?"

"Only ten times a day from the moment I was arrested and right through the trial. But they think I killed him; they weren't about to run plates for me. Janine—Agent Price—I need you."

"So you keep saying. What do you expect me to do, Morgan? You're a convicted murderer and a wanted fugitive. Turn yourself in, and I'll see what I can do."

"While they take another twenty years of my life? I don't think so."

"Damn it, you're gutsy."

"You want to know what I am? I'm scared! Two months ago, I was twenty-three with a few speeding tickets and a bar fight on my record. Now I'm twenty years older, on the run from a murder rap, hobbling from arthritis in my right knee, and almost eligible for AARP. Oh, and by the way, my sometime friend Lonny Myers has been murdered, and they'll probably knock me off next if you or the cops don't grab me first!"

There's a silence while she's either absorbing all this or stalling to get a fix on me. Then I hear the sound of keys being typed. "You sure about those numbers?" she asks.

"Five, four, seven. New luxury sedan. Black."

"I have one possibility here registered to Alikon-Chandler Industrial." Another silence.

"What?"

"Alikon-Chandler is the parent company of Genescence."

"As in TimeLock! Which Lonny went through six weeks ago."

"It's a pool car. Any one of a hundred people could have checked it out. Or you got the plates wrong."

"Let's find out which one of the hundred it was."

"Are you crazy? That's private, corporate information!"

"So, add another five years to my sentence. Just tell me why somebody at Genescence killed Lonny Myers and wants me dead!"

"Genescence and drugs aren't mutually exclusive."

"What does that mean?"

"Lonny could have been into drugs, dealing with somebody at the company."

"Come on, Agent Price. You don't believe that. And we both know I've been on long enough for you to trace this call, but I'm betting you haven't because you know something's going on that's way bigger than me."

"Listen, Morgan. I'm due at a seminar. Take my advice: turn yourself in before this gets any worse for you."

"Exactly how much worse could it get?"

But she's gone.

CHAPTER ELEVEN

I've officially been on the run for three days. Keeping as low a profile as possible, of course. I've tried to reach Janine Price several times, but I think I've worn out my welcome. You know, the one I never had in the first place?

And so, much as I don't want to involve my friends, I realize I could really use their help. Emotional help in the form of moral support and practical help in the form of some much-needed cash.

Late at night, after making sure there were no cops staking out their apartment building, I knock on the door of my closest friends, Ben and Eric. I haven't seen or spoken to them since my last day at QFS, but I'm sure they'll come through for me. We're a team.

A decidedly sleepy Ben answers, and, at first, he doesn't even recognize me.

"Ben, it's me—Morgan."

"Jesus, Morgan. What are you doing here?"

Okay, not the relieved-to-see-me-alive greeting I was hoping for, but I edge inside the apartment and close the door behind me. Now a groggy Eric appears from his bedroom, and his half-shut eyes open wide.

"Morgan? Fuck!"

Again, hardly the reunion I was hoping for. In fact, I can tell right away that these guys are actually afraid of me. Not just because they're suddenly harboring a fugitive, but because I've gone from their contemporary to their elder. I'm not one of them anyone. I'm something strange and alien that should be shunned. As if I've somehow become Nolan Keeler. As if TimeLock itself might be contagious.

Fine, forget the moral support. "Guys, I need some cash."

"You shouldn't be here," Eric says.

"He's right, man. You've got to turn yourself in."

"One problem with that, fellas," I say. "I didn't do it. I go back, and my life's over."

"We can't help you, Morgan," Ben says. "Cops were here before asking if we'd heard from you. They'll ask us again, I'm sure."

"But we won't rat you out," Eric adds.

"Gosh. Thanks, buddy," I say with all the sarcasm I can muster. These guys are unbelievable—not a word about how I am, how I can prove my innocence, where I'm going to stay. Just a palpable yearning to get me out of their apartment in the shortest amount of time possible.

"Listen, I won't bother you again, but I need money. Whatever you can spare."

Ben and Eric look at each other, genuinely unsure what to do. For a moment, all I can feel is anger and hurt, but then both sensations suddenly dissipate as I realize what an untenable position I'm putting them in. Maybe they don't believe I actually committed murder, but they know damn well that I'm a convicted felon on the run and that helping me stay on the run is the very definition of aiding and abetting.

"Listen, guys," I say, "I'm sorry to do this to you. I really am. But I don't have a choice. I didn't kill anyone, and someone is trying to kill me. I just need to stay alive long enough to figure out what's behind it all. You're the only friends I've got right now. *Please!*"

Ben and Eric exchange glances again and nod. I think I've gotten through to them. Eric goes to his room and comes back with three twenty-dollar bills. Ben goes to his wallet on the kitchen table, extracts seventy bucks.

"That's all we have," Ben says.

I doubt it, but I'm in no position to argue.

"And you reached out to my mom, right Ben?"

"No direct contact in case they're listening in. I sent her flowers at work with your message in the card."

"Good thinking. Thanks."

"If they catch you, do us a favor, will you?" Ben says nervously. For a second, I think he's going to add something empathetic along the lines of, "Take care of yourself." Instead, I get this: "Don't mention you saw us, okay?"

I grab the money and walk out the door as my friends look at each other with relief. That just leaves one other possible port of call: my sometime girlfriend over the last two years, Alison Lane. Blond, beautiful, and as disinterested in a serious relationship as I was, she was always there when I needed—or wanted—her.

From the moment we met, in fact, there was a palpable sexual energy between us. In no time, we parlayed that attraction into an uncomplicated and drama-free friendship with benefits that was a perfect fit for two young people more fixated on instant gratification than on long-term commitment.

An hour later, I'm in the lobby of Alison's building. I press her apartment number on the security buzzer and hear her voice saying, "Who is it?"

"Alison, it's me."

"Who?" And now I realize that, like everything else about me, my voice has changed as well. Gone is the youthful resonance she's used to. My voice now is deeper, coarser, weaker. No wonder she doesn't recognize it.

"Morgan."

"Is this some kind of joke? Morgan's in jail."

Obviously, she hasn't heard about my escape from the news or from the police, so I decide not to frighten her with the truth. At least until we're face to face.

"I went through TimeLock, remember? In and out in a few days."

"My God. Morgan, is that really you?"

"In the saggy flesh."

"Ah, what can I do for you?"

Wow. That was rather formal, but then I remember this must be as strange for her as it is for me. "What you can do for me is let me in."

"I don't think that's a good idea. Can you come back tomorrow?"

"No, Alison, I can't come back tomorrow. Just buzz me in. Please?"

"I'll come down."

"Whatever."

A few minutes later, she emerges from the elevator, and then stops dead in her tracks when she sees me. Shocked, she lets out a slasher-movie-worthy gasp.

Despite her reaction to me, I instinctively move toward Alison for a hug, but she actually recoils.

"Don't be scared," I say. "It's still me—just an older me."

"Wait a minute," she says. "I thought you got forty years. You only look twenty-five or thirty years older."

Thanks a lot, I want to say. But instead, I tell her this: "It's twenty. And that's what I want to talk to you about. I got lucky. There was a riot at the prison right when I was being processed, and I managed to escape."

"You're on the run?"

"Big-time. And I need your help."

Alison is visibly shaking, and I realize it can't just be that I've gone through TimeLock and am so many years older than the last time she saw me.

"Alison, I didn't kill Lonny. You believe me, don't you?"

"I did . . . but you were found guilty."

"You think that's the first time an innocent person has been found guilty? Come on. You know I could never hurt anyone. Especially you."

Again, I move toward her, hoping somehow our old attraction will override her fear and confusion. I'm even allowing myself to think that once she's over the trauma of seeing me at forty-three instead of twenty-three, she might let me stay with her for a night or two. Actually, truth be told, for the first time in my relationship with Alison, I don't care about sex—all I really want is a short stay and a long hug.

But it isn't happening. I can understand that Alison's physical attraction to me is gone, but I actually thought she cared about me, at least a little. Instead, what I'm witnessing is Ben and Eric all over again. TimeLock has made me a pariah among my closest friends when I need them most. Sure, on a purely intellectual level, I get it. I may be putting them in the crosshairs of the cops, Lonny's killers, or both. Truth is—I'm not sure I'd be any more welcoming if a suddenly middle-aged escaped killer showed up at *my* doorstep asking for help. But, on a purely emotional level, it still hurts to realize just how alone in the world I really am right now.

"What do you want from me?" Alison asks coldly.

"I was hoping to stay here for a few days until I can figure things out."

"I can't do that, Morgan. I'm sorry, but that would make me an accomplice."

"Okay. Do you have any spare cash lying around?"

"You know I never use cash. Maybe I could pull together ten or twenty dollars, but that's it."

"Never mind."

"Don't be mad. I just can't . . . get involved."

"Of course not," I say bitterly. "Listen, I have to go."

"Take care of yourself, will you?"

"Right. Thanks anyway."

"Sure. See you," she says.

I don't think so. "Goodbye, Alison."

She can't get into the elevator fast enough, and I walk out the front door. Before heading off, I look up at the balcony of Alison's third-floor apartment just in time to see her enter and run into the arms of a shirtless man who doesn't look a day over twenty.

As I walk down the street, I start to cry. I've lost everything. My youth. My friends. My future.

I've never felt more alone.

CHAPTER TWELVE

It's two days later, and I'm quickly running out of both cash and options. I can't spend the rest of my life hiding out in cheap motels and subsisting on fast food. Which is why I've decided to take my biggest chance yet.

I heard on the news about today's gala extravaganza at Genescence, and I knew I had to be there. Right now, my only lead is that Lonny's killers apparently drove to the cabin in a company-owned car. So, crazy at it may seem, I figure this gala is my only chance of getting some face-to-face time with Genescence CEO Patrick Loder and maybe, just maybe, determining his level of culpability. If there is any.

I drive an old van from Lonny's garage up the steep circular driveway approaching the enormous headquarters of Genescence, the proud parent of that bouncing baby affront to God and nature called TimeLock. I approach the entrance, which is throbbing with activity. Posh cars and government limos are swooping up and discharging VIPs. A security guard moves toward the van, but it's not this particular rent-a-cop I'm worried about, it's running into the real thing. Now that I think about it, coming here was a really bad idea.

I show the guard the fake digital ID I created yesterday. Goodbye, Morgan Eberly, escaped convict, and hello, Daniel Price (sorry, Janine—I couldn't resist), an employee of Collier & Collier, the company that's catering today's event.

The guard checks me out and reacts to my attire: T-shirt, windbreaker, jeans. I would have taken better clothes from Lonny, but all he had was what I was already wearing: T-shirt, windbreaker, jeans. The guard continues to look me over skeptically. Rather than trying to con him, I decide to play the pity card instead, posing as a loser in his forties trying to hold on to a job a teenager would turn down and driving a van that's so old it looks like it went through TimeLock with me.

"Sir, I'll be honest with you. I'm already on Mr. Collier's shit list. I'm late, out of uniform, and a little hungover. But I really need this job. I'm all my mom has left." Always good to throw a little grain of truth into the mix.

After a long hesitation, the guard finally nods, says, "You want the service entrance. Just go up there and turn right."

"Thank you, Officer." I know he's not a real officer, but I'd bet anything he likes hearing the word. And sure enough, all of a sudden, he's my new best friend.

"Have a good day," he says, all smiles.

I park the van near a back entrance. Half a dozen panel trucks are disgorging supplies for the party. A number of men are carrying food trays, including me a few moments later. I deposit a tray of cold cuts on a table, but not before stuffing several slices of turkey into my pocket. I hop back in the van and drive around to another entrance blocked by a different security guard.

"Motor pool?" I ask.

"Motor pool?" he responds. "You're going the wrong way. Take the south corridor to the underground garage, level four."

"Level four. Thanks."

Sure enough, level four is a garage that looks like a black luxury sedan dealership. After checking that out, I park the van and head toward the main headquarters of Genescence. Super sleek, super expensive. I spot an entrance marked "Production—S Wing," and peek in to see hundreds of gleaming black capsules. A silent regiment in the half light, stacked in rows like soldiers.

I react to the sound of voices, and soon realize I'm hearing the low murmurs of a small VIP group on a tour. The tour guide is leading her charges past the capsules. She hits a switch, and a control room overlooking the production area is bathed in light.

I didn't risk everything to take a fun-filled tour of TimeLock, but I find myself unable to break away. Plus there's this: the more I learn about the place, the closer I might get to some answers.

Our tour guide is so upbeat and bubbly, you'd think she was welcoming her group to a warped new addition to Disney World. Aging Land. She points toward the left section of the vast room and says, "Over here, we have the original laboratory area where much of the experimental work for TimeLock was carried out. Now, as you can see, it houses the control facilities which direct production."

She leads the way. Curious, I slip into shadows on the fringes of the group. The tour guide directs our attention to the control area, which features a semicircular balcony above, weighted with exotic transformer facilities, computer bases, big-time generators, spaghetti-like clusters of high-voltage cabling, and other heavy equipment.

The lower level consists of banks of flashing computers and a glassed-in room, the outside of which features a complex control panel. As our little tour group pulls up before the room, the guide continues: "And this is the famous laboratory control environment where Genescence made history. Within this room, Dr. Lionel Garvey undertook the first experiments in aging which would lead to TimeLock. These early experiments, of course, were carried out on animals. And let me quickly reassure you—the animals involved were aged only a few weeks and otherwise not harmed in the least. Want to see the process?"

Everyone in the group nods excitedly. To avoid suspicion, I nod as well, though what I'd really like to do is grab the mic from our absurdly peppy tour guide and tell everyone in the room what it's really like to experience the nightmare that is TimeLock up close and personal.

The guide flicks some controls, and rays of light along with a kaleidoscope of powerful beams rain down on a sample display capsule.

"You mean, anything inside would be aging?" asks a middle-aged woman. Or should I say a woman about my age.

Responds the tour guide, "Yes, ma'am. That's where we do our hams."

Everyone laughs. Except me. I'm not *that* good of an actor.

"Now, if you'll come this way, please," the guide says as she leads the group off to another section of the giant room.

I've had enough of this insanity, so I split off and move into the Genescence lobby area. All marble with artsy touches. Clusters of well-dressed guests sip champagne and nibble goodies. I grab a jacket some guy has left draped over a chair at one of the five dozen or so dinner tables that have been set up. A few days ago, this jacket would have fallen off my thin twenty-three-year-old frame. But one of TimeLock's sick little jokes is that it not only ages you in years but in pounds as well. Normally 160, I'm probably 175 by now and, damn it, the jacket's a perfect fit.

I move toward a waiter carrying a tray of champagne glasses and grab a couple of them. "My wife loves the stuff," I tell him to explain the double dipping, but he just forces a fake smile. He couldn't care less.

I spot my target, the great Patrick Loder himself, expensively dressed in the elegant plumage of power. I'd love to approach him, but a guard looks on. And I suspect the room is replete not only with uniformed guards but a good number of undercover police and maybe FBI agents as well, given the caliber of high-profile guests in attendance.

Determined again to blend in, I hang out near a couple of men and react to their conversation as if we're old friends.

"Look, Ed, it may work on a technical level," the first man says, "but what about the socioethical ramifications?"

Responds the other man, "That's irrelevant, Carl. Don't forget—they're helping reduce crime."

"No, they're helping get criminals back on the street."

Janine would love this guy.

Says Ed, "*Ex*-criminals. And you're forgetting something. The recidivism rate among prisoners who go through TimeLock is at a record low."

From behind me, I hear the voice of a woman chime in. "I believe it. Is there anything worse than getting old fast?"

No! I want to shout. And then we're joined by another woman. I'm guessing these are the wives, but all I'm really wondering is when somebody in this self-righteous little foursome is going to wonder who the stranger in jeans and running shoes is.

"Carl's got a point though, don't you think?" the second woman says. "Screwing with nature?"

Responds Carl, "You know what the *Times* called it? 'A crime for the ages.'"

Retorts Ed, "You know what I call that? Liberal bullshit. I say, 'Do the crime, do the time.'"

Someone on the stage clinks a glass, and everyone drifts toward the center of attention—Patrick Loder, Dr. Lionel Garvey, and Governor Myra Winters—all standing on a stage set up in the middle of the room.

"Ladies and gentlemen, distinguished guests, and my valued team members here at Genescence," a "choked up" Loder begins. "Today is . . . whew . . . what a day. There were times when I never thought we'd get here, but we did. Today's the day we celebrate federal approval of Phase Three: twelve more states including Texas and Florida!"

The lobby is filled with the sound of cheers and applause. The world's officially gone mad.

"There are plenty of gods on our Mount Olympus, but only one goddess: Governor Myra Winters!"

Affectionately, Loder reaches out and squeezes the governor's hand.

"It was Governor Winters who put this program into effect. Who pressed its passage in Congress and at the White House. Who drafted the legislation that turned this dream into a reality! Thank you, Governor!"

A beaming Myra Winters basks in the adulation. She says a few words, and, five minutes later, the self-congratulatory love fest is finally over. Curious, I make my way toward Dr. Garvey, not sure how complicit he is in taking out Lonny. In his mid-sixties, Garvey is standing next to a breathtakingly attractive Asian-American woman in her mid-thirties whose name tag reads "Anna Warner."

Garvey is gesturing Loder's way when I hear him say, "God, he's slick."

Responds Anna, "I trusted him more when he was tearing the wings off butterflies."

Garvey nods uneasily, and I get the distinct sense that he's as wary of Patrick Loder as I am.

With that, I now consider the possibility that Dr. Garvey may not be in lockstep with Loder after all. Which hardly means I've found an ally here, only that maybe, just maybe, he might prove useful to me someday.

I make my way to a table with more champagne glasses on it, grab one, and gulp it down just as Myra Winters approaches. I offer her a glass of champagne and she nods. As I hand it to her, she says, "Thanks. Do you work for Genescence?"

"Not exactly," I answer with a half smile. "But I use their products."

The governor stares at me blankly for a moment; she obviously has no idea what I'm talking about. Uninterested in further conversation, she moves off, and, as she does, I feel a powerful hand suddenly clutching my shoulder.

I turn and find myself face to face with a mammoth-sized guard.

"Okay, let's go," he says.

"Take it easy," I tell him, shoving him backward.

"Easy my ass, you son of a bitch!"

He tugs, and I struggle to pull free. The guard hauls out a club.

I smile and say, "Now, is that any way to treat your elders?"

At which moment, I punch him square in the jaw, which I'm sure hurts me far more than it hurts him. And the next thing you know, we're rolling across the marble, guests flying, some screaming. Then Loder appears and gestures for the guard to move aside.

Believe it or not, this is exactly what I was hoping for.

CHAPTER THIRTEEN

"**W**ho are you?" Loder shouts at me.

"Frank Myers. It's about my son's murder."

A few minutes later, I'm in Loder's office, trailed by three guards, including the one I just did the two-step with out in the lobby. To my surprise, though, Loder waves them all out, though not before stopping one of them and saying, "Ask Mr. Colby to join us."

The musclemen all exit, only to be replaced by a far more imposing figure, impossibly well-built and in his early thirties. His crew cut alone could beat the crap out of me.

Says Loder, "Neil, this is Frank Myers. Mr. Colby is our director of security. Now, how may we help you, Mr. Myers?"

"It's about something that happened in April. My son, Lonny, was killed, but I think they arrested the wrong man. It's true my boy had some scrapes with the law, but he was a good kid. Three months ago, he goes through TimeLock, and four weeks later, he's dead. Problem is—I know the young man they convicted for killing him, and I just don't buy it."

"And why is that?" says Loder.

"He saw another car following Lonny. A Genescence car."

"Do you know whose car?"

"Only that it was checked out of the pool. That's what I was trying to find out."

"I see . . ."

"He told all this to the police?" Colby asks.

I nod. "But they didn't believe him."

"So, you turned yourself into a detective," says Loder in an even tone that's neither sympathetic nor menacing.

"A detective who has no problem breaking and entering," Colby adds.

"Well," says Loder tolerantly, "let's just call it crashing a party, shall we, Neil?"

The truth is—much as I can't stand Loder's slickness, and much as this guy Colby looks like he just graduated with honors from Evil Henchman U—there's a small chance these guys are in the dark about Lonny, me, and the cabin. Which is precisely why I came here in the first place. And then there's this to consider: if they *were* mixed up with it all, they'd have to know who I was, and we wouldn't be having this delightful conversation.

"How'd you know it was a Genescence vehicle?" Colby asks me.

I'm ready for this one too. "Checked it out with a guy I know at the DMV."

"Let me have those numbers."

"NTT547."

Colby moves to a computer, and he hits some keys.

"Here it is: Internal update, Motor Pool Department, Stolen vehicle—VIN 468092134-988745, license plate Maryland NTT547."

A newly chummy Loder says, "Well, there's part of your explanation, Mr. Myers. May I call you Frank? I'm sorry to add to your grief, but your son had stolen one of our vehicles. He wasn't being followed by one of our sedans; he was driving it."

Bullshit. So Loder and Colby are in this up to their necks. They know exactly who I am and why I'm here. They let me walk right into the lion's den to see what

I know and who I've told, which makes me every bit as disposable as the prepaid phone in my pocket. The one thing I have going for me is the fact that half of Washington's elite, including Loder's precious client Myra Winters, are twenty-five feet away, and the last thing these two want is a scene.

Forcing a smile that just doesn't belong on his granite face, Colby eases me out of the office with this: "Sorry if we came down hard. That's our job."

He extends a hand. His right hand, of course, but I can see he's a lefty; his watch is on his right wrist. And it glints—the same titanium watchband I saw at the cabin.

"I'm so sorry for your loss, Frank." Loder says. "Tell you what. Take a plate of shrimp home on me."

"Gee, thanks, Patrick," I say. "May I call you Patrick?"

Loder produces a cobra-like smile and shows me out.

It's dark outside when I emerge and head toward my borrowed van. I climb in and shut the door. Now that we're away from the festivities, I'm hardly surprised to see Colby and several guards racing toward me. No way are they letting me leave this place alive.

"Okay, Mr. Eberly, out you go." Colby shouts. As planned, they can't see through the tinted windows. Colby tries the door—nothing. He then smashes the window and yanks open the door. But I'm not in the driver's seat.

The van's rear doors open, and I come flying out atop Lonny's motorcycle. Colby and his goons fire at me, but the bike is too fast. I rush down the driveway and am beyond relieved to see the main gate opening up to let a limo in. I speed downhill, pass the limo, and roar off into the night.

CHAPTER FOURTEEN

It's four days later, and I'm holed up in a different sleazebag motel. I'm finished with the dumb for a while. No walking right into Loder's evil lair. No playing undercover spy. No venturing outside except for food.

Needless to say, confinement and inactivity don't sit well with me. The ADD is kicking in big-time, and it's all, of course, magnified a thousandfold by the fear that I'll spot Colby or the cops headed my way any minute.

This forced downtime has also given me ample opportunity to explore the one emotion other than terror that defines my existence right now: melancholy. The source of the sadness is obvious—twenty years of my life have been stolen from me. The best twenty. I was just starting to grow up enough to consider pursuing a serious relationship for the first time, even marriage and fatherhood. Now the odds are that I won't live long enough to experience either.

The brutal reality is that even if I were exonerated tomorrow, I could never pick up where I left off. Not with my friends or the girls I've dated, and maybe not even with my mother, all of whom would invariably regard me as some kind of freak much like Ben, Eric, and Alison do. The Elephant Man in the room.

Finally, I snap out of my depression and tune in to the news. And it fills me with another emotion I've become quite acquainted with lately: fury. Because the program that took my friend's life and prematurely aged me twenty years is fast becoming a runaway hit.

Anchor Gene Wheeler is on camera, with images of White House picketers in the background.

"One year in, and the country remains sharply divided along party lines, but the polls are starting to tilt in the president's favor. Many question the morality of TimeLock, but few can argue with the results. Every one of the states that has adopted the program has not only seen reduced prison overcrowding, but significant reductions in crime as well. Now only two key questions remain. First: Will this highly divisive program eventually become the law of the land? And second: Will the success of TimeLock catapult a once political unknown, Governor Myra Winters of Maryland, into the White House?"

The prospect of this abomination going nationwide fills me with rage and a new determination to bring TimeLock to its knees. Which means I'm done sitting, I'm done waiting, and I'm done hiding.

I mute the TV and grab one of my prepaid phones. This time, Janine picks right up.

"Hello?"

"Your favorite fugitive."

"I meant to ask you last time—how the hell did you get my cell number?"

"I'm a computer genius, remember?"

"It's been a few days. I figured you'd be long gone by now."

"Just laying low for a while."

"I heard about your little coming-out party at Genescence. Did you really think they wouldn't know who you are? The famous con who stepped out of one of their capsules and walked out through the front door?"

"I had to take a chance. Figured even if Loder recognized me, he wouldn't want a scene on his big day. I was wrong. Listen—I have to talk to you."

"Damn it, Morgan. You're a real pain in the ass, you know that? Do yourself a favor, and end this now."

I react to a sound outside. I open the curtain and see a police car in the motel parking lot. Shit. But it drives off, and I let out a sigh of relief.

"Okay," I say.

"Okay, what?" asks Janine.

"I'll turn myself in. But only to you. And first, you help me for twenty-four hours. If we don't find anything, I'm all yours."

"Gee, Morgan, how can I say no? I harbor an escaped killer and throw away my entire career in law enforcement so you can chase down some crazy conspiracy theory and I can . . . wait—what is it I get out of this again?"

"Maybe the truth about a program you hate as much as I do."

There's a long pause. "Morgan, tonight happens to be the annual interagency affair at the Potomac Club, and I'm late."

"I think you'll want to hear this. I got through to the big cheese himself—Loder. He brings in his security chief, Colby. And guess who Colby is? One of the guys who chased me at the cabin. One of the guys who shot Lonny Myers."

"And how exactly do you know all that?"

"Because Colby was wearing the watch I saw that night. Bright metal, expensive titanium."

"Titanium? That's your big 'evidence?'"

"The car's out of Genescence. This guy's wearing the same kind of watch. Oh, and they tried to kill me—again."

"Talk about burying the lead! What do you mean, they tried to kill you again?"

"At the party, at Genescence. While Loder was schmoozing with the hoi polloi, Colby and his merry band of assassins were trying to blow me away. Fortunately, I came prepared just in case. But, no, I don't have proof, so don't bother asking."

"Get some, and we'll talk."

"By the time I do, I won't be in any condition to talk."

And she's gone. I stare off in frustration, then freeze when I see what's on CNN now: a photo of my fellow TimeLock escapee Calvin Perry, then footage of him in a football game making a game-winning play.

I unmute the television in time to hear this: "In happier times, of course, Perry played for Cleveland and later for Tampa. Cause of death is still uncertain at this time, but the charred remains of his body were found in a remote part of Florida, five days after he and two others escaped from Loomis Detention Center in the middle of their TimeLock processing."

So, Rajek and I weren't the only ones who got out! But more to the point—why was Perry killed, why were the remains burned just like Lonny's, and how long will it be before I go up in flames too? I try Janine again several times, but no luck. Which means it's time for us to reunite the old-fashioned way: up close and personal.

CHAPTER FIFTEEN

Okay, I'm back to dumb. When I sashayed into the Genescence party, I still wasn't sure whether Loder was involved in Lonny's death. Well, now I know.

But I can be absolutely certain that the people at the party I'm about to crash tonight *definitely* want to nail my ass. Yes, as you may have guessed, I'm actually at the Potomac Yacht Club, hoping to win over Agent Price, but resigned to the likelihood that the FBI will have me back in a TimeLock capsule before the week is over.

Still, I have to take the chance. I can't keep hiding forever, and, at this point, I'd rather be in FBI custody than running from Loder and Colby for the rest of my life. Given the choice, I'll take Janine's at least somewhat friendly fire over Colby's literal fire any day.

I make my way into the corner of the private dining room reserved for FBI and other Justice Department employees. Not surprisingly, I'm confronted by a guard. By this point, I think I've met every security guard east of the Mississippi.

"I'll need an ID and a reservation number, sir," the guard says.

No way can I fake ID my way into this particular gathering, so I go a different way. "No, I was just passing by. Thought I should tell you there's a Chevrolet Malibu on fire in the back lot. DC plates." The Feds love their Chevy Malibus.

The guard scurries off toward some guests, and I scoot out the back door to a garden area also reserved for the same party. A band plays, and a few couples are dancing. I look around for Janine, then finally spot her awkwardly dancing with a square-jawed man in his forties who looks like Mr. FBI: stiff, humorless, boring. Of course, that's just guesswork since I have no idea who he is. Or could it be wishful thinking? Damn, Janine looks stunning tonight.

Now a voice can be heard over the PA system: "We understand there may be a Chevrolet Malibu with DC plates on fire in the rear parking lot."

Mr. FBI stops dancing and gestures to Janine that he'll be right back. In fact, four other agents are right behind him.

I sneak up behind Janine and whisper, "Hi there. Remember me?"

She reacts, wide-eyed, pushes me back behind some shrubbery. "What are you doing here?"

"Dancing lessons. What do you think? I had to talk to you."

"Damn it, this is an agency function! What's stopping me from arresting you right here?"

"You tell me."

"God, you look like shit. And don't you ever shave?"

"You look beautiful."

She glares my way. "It's important," I say.

"You have thirty seconds, or everyone here except the bartender will be reading you your rights."

"I was watching TV right after we talked. And this story came on about Calvin Perry getting murdered."

"Thank you for sharing. Who's Calvin Perry?"

"Played pro football. Then he started to drink and the rest of it, went down the tubes, took to drug trafficking, ended up in the can, went through my class at the TimeLock Academy."

She gestures for me to get on with it.

"Here's the cast: Lonny, Calvin Perry, me. Two out of three are dead. The third one they tried to kill. Twice. 'They' being, in my humble opinion, at least one guy at Genescence, driving a company car and pretty high up: the aforementioned Neil Colby, head of security."

"How many people in your processing group?"

"About fifteen. And if you're doing 'odds' again, two murders and one attempt is kind of off the charts, don't you think?"

"Yes, except Lonny wasn't in your group, so what's your point?" she asks, her eyes darting around, no doubt waiting for her dance partner to return any second.

"Come on, Janine. Agent Price. You know what my point is. Something's all fucked up with the program."

She frowns, and if I'm reading her right, she knows what I'm saying is undeniable.

"So, are we partners?" I ask.

"In what?"

"Well, you know, I always thought it would be kind of fun to work with the FBI."

"Golly, Morgan. Why didn't you say so before? I'd hate for you to miss out on all that *fun*, but you don't have anything. Forget the FBI and the police. You don't have enough for the Boy Scouts."

I decide to go all in—nothing to lose, right? "So, we kind of go at it unofficially. Look, maybe Genescence wants to shut three guys up: me, Lonny Myers, and Calvin Perry. Who knows why? Or maybe they want to shut everybody up, the whole class of thirty-two."

"That's only half the issue. The other half is *why*."

And then I hear her say the magic words that tell me she's in: "And how exactly would you 'unofficially' go about this?"

"We go to my place . . . I mean—where I used to work. Nobody will be there this time of night, and I know their computer system inside out."

Janine's partner returns. She gestures for me to wait and moves toward her companion.

"False alarm," the man says. "Guess some joker saw all the Chevy Malibus out there and thought he'd pull a fast one."

Janine throws me a knowing glare. "Hey! Look who's here!" the man says excitedly. I peer out from my make-shift hiding place past some bushes and spot none other than Governor Myra Winters making a grand entrance.

She's accompanied by a couple of flunkies and is greeted with oohs and ahhs and a smattering of applause.

"Don't move. I want you to meet her!" the man tells Janine, and he hurries off. He knows the governor well enough for big huggies and escorts her over. Two of the three most important women in my life are about to meet. This should be good.

"May I present Governor Myra Winters? Governor, this is my colleague, Agent Janine Price."

"Agent Price," Winters says flatly.

Janine's response is a withering glare and a cold, "Nice to meet you."

Governor Winters is not oblivious, but turns back to the man and says, "Don't forget the TimeLock rally, Walter—Friday night at Greenbriar. The veep's handling keynote."

"I'll be there," the fawning Walter responds. A couple approaches Governor Winters and chats her up, which gives Walter the opportunity to say to Janine, "What was the cold shoulder all about?"

"I don't like TimeLock, Walter."

"So I've heard. From now on, keep it to yourself, Janine. I mean it."

He heads off to rejoin Myra Winters as Janine moves

back toward me. I gesture to the governor and quip, "I can't go to a party these days without running into her."

"I can't do this, Morgan."

Now I point at Walter. "What's up with Mr. Excitement?"

"His patience. Let's get out of here."

An hour later, I'm driving a car I was forced to temporarily borrow from a local repair shop after abandoning Lonny's van at Genescence. No way could Janine take the chance of someone seeing me in her car, so she reluctantly agreed to join me in this one. For obvious reasons, I forget to tell my already-conflicted FBI agent passenger that this particular vehicle is stolen.

"While we're on the subject of Walter—are we talking 'Mr. Right?' or just 'Mr. Right Wing?'"

"There's nothing wrong with law and order. And Walter Greene happens to be a very nice man."

"Who bores you to tears."

"Where do you get that?" Janine fumes.

"You couldn't wait to get away from him."

"Stop the car!"

I screech to a stop on a bridge crossing the Potomac. A steaming Janine struggles to push the door open and says, "This was a mistake."

"I think the latch is broken," I tell her. "Cheap rental. I'll have to go around." But I pause a moment to say this, and I mean every word: "Don't go. I apologize. I have no right meddling in your business. Especially since you're putting your career on the line for me."

She reacts with a scoff.

"Okay, not for me. For TimeLock. Anyway, sorry if I sound like an idiot. Guess I'm a little jumpy. Guess I'm not as old and wise as I look."

Janine slowly refastens her belt and smiles. "Wise, no. Old, yes."

I smile too. "Thanks."

We drive off and bask in our silent rapprochement. Until I say, "But you've got to admit he's boring."

Janine glares at me with exasperation and just possibly the slightest hint of a smile.

CHAPTER SIXTEEN

It's the middle of the night, and Janine and I are huddled in my old cubicle at QuickRight Financial Services. This is do-or-die time for me—literally. I log on to a secure network and do my virtuoso keyboard moves as Janine looks on.

"Okay," she says. "What's your brilliant idea?"

"If all the dots connect, then this guy Colby must have been in Florida. Where Calvin Perry was killed."

"Checking hotels?"

"Airlines. I don't think he'd stick around long enough to take a room."

I type in, "Passenger sweep; all airlines; Colby, Neil; Wash DC/Miami." The search is almost instantaneous, and the result is beyond disappointing: NOT FOUND. But Janine chimes in with the obvious: "He wouldn't be dumb enough to use his own name, Morgan."

"But he might have used Genescence to make the reservation," I say hopefully.

I hit the keys again and "Reservation made by Genescence" comes up on the screen, followed by "All airlines" and "Wash. DC/Miami." Again, the computer searches data, whips into a blur, and once more comes up with NOT FOUND.

"Wait a minute," I say rather loudly. Janine gestures for me to keep it down, though nobody else is here. "This guy Colby is pretty high up."

"You mean he sent his flunkies?"

"That, too, but what I meant was company jet."

"Okay, but if that's the case, how do you access flight information?"

"How about FAA?"

"You can't go into a federal agency for flight information! That's a felony!"

"So is murder."

With a look of complete exasperation on her face, Janine says, "What bugs me is that sometimes you make sense."

On the monitor, a flood of FAA logging info comes up. Now I type in "Arrival/Miami/Genescence/9/6–9/8/." The computer runs through hundreds of entries, then highlights: "Genescence/Lear KT9297/arr 9/7 0600/ dep 9/7 1100/."

Janine and I exchange looks. "Bingo!" I say.

"Colby was there! No, that's circumstantial. The plane was there."

"Right. The plane taxied across town, ran over Calvin Perry, set him on fire, and tippy-toed out."

If looks could kill. Then it hits me. I start typing again. "I'm tapping into the Bureau of Prisons. Let's check out my teammates."

Janine rolls her eyes. "Also illegal. But I've taken such a headfirst dive into the cesspool, I suppose it doesn't matter now."

On the screen a list comes up under the heading "Processing Groups—Loomis." Among the names, of course: Eberly, Morgan. Then Calvin Perry, Charlie Rajek, Kyle Bannon, and a few others I don't recognize.

"Wait," I say. "This won't help us. Only Perry, Rajek, and I made it out. We know what happened to Perry. Rajek I've already tried to track down—nothing yet. All the rest still have another couple of weeks at Loomis."

"Right," Janine says. "What we need to find out is what happened to the guys in Lonny's group, the first ones processed. The ones who already got out."

I smile at her. "I knew you'd come around."

"What are you talking about?"

"What 'we' need to find out. Like I said, partners."

"Fuck off."

"And we're back."

I start typing again, and a new list comes up.

"They could be all over the country by now," Janine says. "You need a central registry."

"Right. We'll just go into the FBI."

"What? You can't do that!"

"Hold it! Aren't you a federal agent? Aren't you with the FBI? Don't you want this information too?"

"Jesus, Morgan. What am I doing here? You're an escaped convict, and I'm risking everything I've worked for my entire life. Three generations of law enforcement—did I mention that? The first woman in my family to join the bureau. Top of my class. Nearly perfect record. Now the whole thing is circling the drain because of some unshaven, low-rent, bad-boy biker wannabe."

I smile. Meanwhile, to Janine's shock, I've managed to backdoor into the FBI during her little speech. The monitor reads, "FBI—Confidential," along with a list of the names and last known locations of the guys in the very first TimeLock processing group—Lonny's group. Janine looks heavenward in complete annoyance, but a moment later, her curiosity takes over.

"I take it we're seeing if they wound up as dead as Lonny and Calvin Perry."

"Exactly," I say. "No wonder you were top of your class."

"I'll try to remember that when I'm waving to you from the next capsule."

"Okay, let's see what happened to our little freshman group."

Another flurry on the screen. When it settles into focus, seven names are highlighted.

Janine starts reading the info out loud. "Wilkins, Ned, New York City. Killed in an apartment fire in Houston ten days after his release. Andrade, Phillip. Drowned in a boating accident in North Carolina two weeks after getting out. Body never recovered. Kenner, Tom, missing, presumed dead while hiking in Northern California a week after Loomis. Body also never recovered. Barton, Fred, burnt to death in a meth lab accident in Philadelphia four days after his release. Amici, Vincent . . ."

"Amici—I remember him! They trotted him on stage like a poster boy for the program." I read off the screen. "Committed suicide by jumping off the Potomac River Bridge. Let me guess. Body never recovered."

Something has changed in Janine's demeanor. She's finally ready to put everything on the line for me. I mean, for TimeLock.

"Now what?" I ask, the reasonable one for a change. "Isn't it all, as you would say, still circumstantial?"

"We keep digging. We'll find something."

"Something like Colby slicing me open on national television."

She smiles. "That would help. The question is: what's the level of authority? Colby?"

"Colby wears a crew cut," I say. As though that explains it all, which, in a way, it does. "No, like I told you, I track this all the way to the top man himself, Patrick Loder. No way Colby tried to knock me off at the party without Loder's say-so."

"Morgan, you'd better stay with me tonight, play it safe."

"I thought you'd never ask," I joke, though Janine—not surprisingly—isn't laughing.

CHAPTER SEVENTEEN

Although Janine comes off as something of a mini-malist—stark clothes (last night's black gown notwithstanding), no-nonsense demeanor, and (until meeting me) a strict by-the-books adherence to the law—her condo is surprisingly colorful. Artistic, even. Prints by Wassily Kandinsky (considered a pioneer in abstract art, I am promptly informed upon arrival) dot the walls, pottery collections fill the living room, and there are enough plants to open up a flower shop.

I'm impressed. And beyond grateful we couldn't go back to my dump of an apartment where the closest thing to fine art is the Three Stooges screensaver on my laptop.

Lying on Janine's sofa the next morning, I find myself feeling oddly pensive, wondering whether TimeLock has matured me in ways that aren't just physical. Despite my life hanging by a thread and the fact that my incredibly risky (albeit strangely exciting) little investigative sojourn with Janine may come to a crashing halt any minute, I feel amazingly calm, a whole new sensation for me. It's as if I've somehow evolved beyond the teen angst that has defined my life for as long as I can remember.

And there's something else. Before TimeLock, I wouldn't have looked twice at a woman like Janine Price. Well, I would have looked, but, in my dumb, sexist way, I probably would have found her too serious and intimidating to ever ask out—not that she would have said yes anyway.

After all, most of the girls I've dated over the years were like me—more interested in partying than figuring out their grand purposes in life. By contrast, Janine is obviously someone who's always known who she was and what she wanted. Which will make me feel all the more guilty if I'm the one who brings everything she's worked for crashing to the ground.

I'm startled by a thumping noise, and, wrapped in a blanket, I peek into Janine's bedroom to find her loping along on a treadmill in leggings and a skin-tight top. I'm in no rush to look away, and, after a couple of seconds, she becomes aware of my somewhat leering presence. Unfazed, she glances over and says, "Morning. How'd you sleep?"

"Alone," I joke. "How many miles?"

"Ten."

"That's *too* healthy. You can get sick being in that kind of shape."

"You ought to try it. That's why you're soft."

She stops the treadmill, gets off.

"Soft? Where do you get soft? Five months back, I came in third in a fifteen-mile charity run."

"Five months back was twenty years ago."

I produce my best fake smile, then gesture to the treadmill, asking whether she minds if I try. She nods, I retrieve my sneakers from the other room, then realize I only have jeans to wear—not exactly prime running attire. So, I lose the blanket, find a towel and jump on the treadmill. I'll show her. I fire it up to 6.5 and start running. A minute later, the towel flies off, and I realize that, other than my sneakers, I'm stark naked.

I expect Janine to be annoyed, disgusted, or flustered, but she's cool and collected as usual. Considering

I'm hanging out there for all the world to see, I actually would have preferred *some* kind of reaction. So, I decide to be as indifferent to my nakedness as she is and start talking.

"This is the first normal thing I've done in weeks," I say breathlessly. "If you call an escaped murderer running naked on an FBI agent's treadmill normal."

Now sweating and huffing profusely, I can barely get the words out. Janine moves toward the treadmill, lowers the speed to a walk. And glances ever so briefly at my exposed apparatus.

"Like I said—soft."

I step off the treadmill, wrap the towel around me and say, "I used to run for thirty minutes and barely work up a sweat. Now look at me."

"I believe I just did," Janine says with a slightly mischievous grin.

I smile, and then, seemingly out of nowhere, it hits me. "I just remembered! Charlie Rajek, one of the guys who escaped that day. The one I couldn't find? He's a short-order cook."

"Okay, that was random. You know where he used to work?"

"No idea."

"Doesn't matter, does it? I mean . . . it's not like he would go back to his old job."

"Or use his real name. But he did mention maybe asking a brother-in-law for help when we were both on the run from Loomis. Some kind of restaurant maybe? Blue Link? Blue Trails?"

"Blue Lakes Resort?"

"That's it! Worth a shot."

A couple of hours later, we're riding up to Blue Lakes Resort, a complex of low-slung buildings, bungalows, tennis courts, riding trails, kiddie rides, and restaurants.

Having returned the car I temporarily stole to the repair shop and still being nervous about driving together in Janine's government-issued sedan, we're actually on Lonny's motorcycle.

We secure the bike in front of a coffee shop and dismount. Janine rubs her rear as if she'd had a rough ride.

"You'll get used to it," I say.

"I'll get used to it, my ass," she growls.

"That's what I said. Your ass will get used to it."

"Very funny."

There's a kitchen beyond a short-order grill area. I approach the grill man. "Charlie Rajek around?"

Then I remember that we have no idea what name Rajek is using these days. I take out a picture of him I downloaded from the FBI files.

"This guy. But older."

"On his break," the man says. "Check the employee lounge."

He mumbles some directions, and we make our way to the lounge, a large room with furniture from the Carter administration. Empty. But then Janine and I react to the sound of hard breathing behind a sofa. We move toward the couch and discover the sprawled figure of Charlie Rajek on the floor behind it. His body is twisted, and so are his features. But his eyes are wide open, and we drop beside him.

"Charlie, it's Morgan Eberly. What is it?"

"Started this morning," Rajek struggles to answer. "Went away, but now it's back. Can't move."

Janine looks at me, mouths the word *paralyzed*?

"We've got to get you to a hospital."

Suddenly, Rajek trembles. His body remains rigid, legs stiff, hands clawed, but he seems to vibrate. Helpless, I whip off my windbreaker and throw it over him as if that will help. It doesn't. The vibration continues, his glazed eyes staring straight ahead. And then, remarkably, the intensity level escalates. It's as though he's in the grip of some gigantic creature that's violently shaking him and refusing to let go.

Silent as death, his eyes showing terror, Rajek stares eerily ahead. His face contorts, his skin creases.

"Jesus," I gasp.

"Oh my God," Janine says.

Rajek's affliction is age. He's aging before our very eyes. His skin becomes leather, his eyes turn milky. His hair starts to turn gray, then yellowish white. It begins to fall out, first hair by hair, then in clumps. His scalp takes on the spotted lesions of advanced age. The facial pits, crags, sores, and discoloration of old age erupt like the volcanic surface of a primitive world. There is one last furious outbreak of quavering. Then he's still.

"Guess his time was up." It's Colby, joined by two guys I don't recognize who are both holding guns with attached silencers.

One of the men is carrying a large, folded duffle bag. And while Janine and I are still horrified over Rajek's transformation, Colby and his cohorts seem to be taking it in stride.

"Is that what happens to everybody who goes through?" I ask Colby.

"One in three. Your friend Myers was my first. I caught up with him at your cabin just before *this* happened," he says as he nods to Rajek's body. "Look at it this way: there are bound to be kinks in the first bunch off the line."

"You really care. That's nice," I say.

Colby smirks. "I was just thinking about the one-in-three odds, you know? If it weren't for your proclivity for being at the wrong place at the wrong time—like showing up here today—you'd have had a pretty good chance."

"And was I in the wrong place at the wrong time at the cabin, or did you always plan on framing me for killing Lonny?"

"No—if anything, you were an unwanted complication. We were following your friend. You weren't on our radar at all—until recently, of course. But, hey, I'm thinking it's all working out pretty well for us, wouldn't you agree?"

"Hey, Neil, you know what *I'm* thinking? You've probably got a family and two curly-headed little kids you read stories to, but my hunch is you're a piece of shit."

Yeah, that should bring him to his knees. Colby gestures toward Janine. "Who's she?"

No answer. He nods to one of the men and, in a frighteningly calm—even polite—tone, says, "Check her bag, Mr. Coombs."

The man grabs Janine's purse, examines it, and comes up with her ID. "FBI." Coombs says it with surprise and shows it to Colby, who's no less taken aback. He then takes her cell phone and demands mine as well.

Colby moves toward Janine. "You were in on the arrest. Then it got personal, and now he's got you running around like his dutiful sidekick?"

Colby gestures to Coombs, and he again digs into the purse then shakes his head. No gun.

Colby nods in satisfaction. Again, he signals. Coombs moves to Janine. He gropes every inch of her body, squeezes her breasts with detachment. No gun.

"Where is it?" Colby barks.

"I'm off duty," Janine replies.

Colby's skeptical, but lets it pass. "Mr. Coombs, Mr. Tyler," he says to the two men, "time to go." The two henchmen grab the large duffle bag. They unfold it alongside Rajek's body, open the long zipper. They roll Rajek into the bag, zip it up. Colby waves his gun. "Let's go."

"Where?" I ask, but I'd rather not hear the answer.

CHAPTER EIGHTEEN

Our group emerges from the employee lounge, and we run into four resort employees. Colby has to hide his gun by slipping it into his jacket pocket. Janine suddenly grabs one of the employees and screams, "Don't go in there! We've got a rat infestation! These guys are the exterminators. Look how many they caught!"

The employees look at the duffle bag Tyler and Coombs are carrying, filled with what must be a hundred rats. They check out the "exterminators" in their nicely tailored suits, and, somehow, it seems to make sense: management disguising the exterminators to hold down the panic. I chime in with an equally panicked, "Come on! We better go ahead and clear the area!"

This shouldn't make any sense at all to them, but groupthink takes over, and, suddenly, we're all breaking into a run.

I hear Colby tell his hit squad to get rid of the body, and they move off. A little farther, and we'll be free of them. A few yards later, Janine and I break off from the four employees and run toward the lakeshore. Breathless, we dash behind some foliage to regroup.

Says Janine, "Okay. You were right about him. The one with the watch. He's a pro. Private security here won't be worth a damn against him."

And I ask the question that I've been wanting to ask since we were in the employee lounge. "Where *is* the gun?"

"Home, for God's sake."

"Swell."

A few minutes later, with no goons in sight, we make our way back to Lonny's motorcycle, climb aboard, and speed off. But not before seeing Colby race out of hiding and run toward another parked bike. He breaks the lock, works some wires, hops on, starts it up, and chases after us.

Janine is a highly trained agent, and I'm hardly a novice at riding a motorcycle, but she didn't train on a beat-up Kawasaki, and I'm not the fearlessly agile twenty-three-year-old I was a week ago. And as we reach a crowded city street, Colby is gunning toward us like the Terminator.

"Morgan! Please try not to kill us!" she implores.

Putting up a false front, I shout, "Don't worry. I'm pretty good at this."

As Colby closes in, weapon in hand, I decide we only have one incredibly stupid, unbelievably risky move left, so I gun the bike down the stairs of a subway entrance. Don't try this at home, kids.

Right on cue, Janine shouts, "What the fuck are you doing?"

"Seeing how good *he* is."

"That's a relief," she yells back. "I was afraid it was something stupid!"

We bounce down the stairs as commuters fly in every direction to avoid us. Seconds later, Colby's bike comes barreling toward us.

I crash the cycle right through a gate next to the turnstiles and down another row of stairs toward the subway platform, Colby following suit. Seeing Colby is right behind us, I make a tough decision and veer the bike over the side and onto the subway tracks.

I can only hope this crazy move will deter Colby, but no such luck: he does the same.

We speed along on the subway tracks, hoping against hope that Colby won't catch us, and a subway train won't crush us. There's one tiny consolation: the bouncing is keeping Colby from getting off a clean shot.

And then we hear it. A train approaching, of course. But from where?

Our bike approaches a split, and now we spot the train, speeding toward us from the left. We swerve onto the track on the right, and a few yards behind, Colby does the same. He fires off a few more shots, and they just miss us, his aim now better adjusted for the rough ride.

We react to the sound of another subway train closing in.

"Morgan, behind us!" Janine shouts.

I look back for a second. Uh oh. But we've just made it to the next station, so I stop the bike. We jump off and desperately climb to the platform as dozens of shocked bystanders look on. As we race off, we look back to see Colby's bike appear. He, too, clambers off and lifts himself to safety. In his case, at the very last second, just as the subway train crashes into the two motorcycles, and metal debris and tires go flying all

126

over the place. Fortunately, while the bikes are goners, the people aboard and near the train appear shaken but otherwise unharmed.

Janine and I rush up the subway stairs and down the street. It's pouring, and I'm breathless, another reminder that I'm not twenty-three anymore. We pause.

Janine turns to me, and, in a mocking sing-song voice, says, "'Let's take my motorcycle to Blue Lakes,' he says. 'It'll be fun,' he says." Then, dead serious: "Look out!"

She tugs me out of sight as Colby emerges from the subway stop. He looks around, then heads off in the opposite direction.

"Let's go," Janine says in her best FBI voice.

"Where are we going?"

"Not we. Me."

CHAPTER NINETEEN

Two hours later, Janine is in a heated argument with Walter Greene in his office. Against her better judgment, but bowing to my insatiable curiosity, she's gone into the meeting with her phone on and me listening in on mine. We would have gotten here sooner, but first we had to replace the cell phones Colby took. In any case, considering our friend Walter could determine the course of my entire life, I still don't think it was too big of an ask that I be allowed to eavesdrop on their meeting.

"I didn't make it up, Walter!" Janine is saying loudly.

"Wild car chases, hopping on and off of motorcycles, enough gunfire for a Saturday morning cartoon—none of which you can substantiate—along with a crazy story about a TimeLock prisoner wrinkling into old age and dying in front of your eyes. Oh, and you had a high-profile fugitive in custody and let him get away. Anything else?"

"For God's sake, Walter, get your head out of Myra Winters's ass!"

I almost blow my cover and laugh into the phone at that line.

"Your precious program is all fucked up!" Janine adds. She then pauses for a moment and continues in a much calmer voice. "Walter, I'm sorry. I was bringing him in, but then we saw what happened to Rajek, and they tried to kill us. Actually, Morgan saved my life."

"So it's 'Morgan' now? And was it 'Morgan' when he was at the Potomac Club last night?"

Oh, boy. The man's in love with her. Not exactly a boon to the chances of him helping me.

Janine adds, "I wanted to check out his story first, and he's on to something. Something big. Listen, I hate the program, and you're all for it. Okay. This is America. But something frightening is going on, and you've got to deal with it!" After a long beat, Janine forcefully says, "Damn it, Walter—take a stand!"

"How about this, Agent Price: your suspension starts as of this minute. A formal hearing will take place in the next week. In the meantime, hand over your badge right now!"

Oh, shit. Janine has just done the hardest thing she ever had to do. And it's all my fault.

CHAPTER TWENTY

Well, as fate would have it, now it's *my* turn to do the hardest thing I've ever had to do.

It's later that night, and Janine has made sure the house isn't being watched. So she and I step into the yard and knock on the back door.

Janine had called earlier, so my mother is expecting us.

Janine walks in first, introduces herself to my mom, then leaves the room to give us privacy. I edge in slowly, giving her as much time as she needs to adjust to her suddenly twice-as-old son.

Finally, I'm in, and she looks me over. I don't know whether she'll faint or scream or cry, but I'm ready for any of it. I think.

After a long beat, she smiles and says, "You bring a girl home to your mother in those filthy clothes?" I laugh, and we run toward each other and wordlessly hug for a full minute. She guides me toward the kitchen table.

"You hungry?" she asks.

"No, they already served us dinner at three at the old-age home." She smiles, and I say, "Yeah, I'm starved. I'm sure Janine is too."

What every mother wants to hear. As she looks me over again, my mom starts to make some sandwiches, then says, "You feel all right?"

"It's weird, Ma. In some ways, I'm the same, yet everything is different. Aging is supposed to be gradual, so how can anyone possibly be prepared for its sudden onslaught?"

"Especially if you did nothing wrong to deserve it. It's not right, and it's not fair. You had your whole life ahead of you, and then . . ."

And now the tears flow. From both of us. Fortunately, Janine only told my mom part of the story, the part about my miraculous escape from Loomis and Janine's efforts to clear my name. If my mother knew I have half of Genescence gunning for me, or that there's a one-in-three chance I very well may go all Dorian Gray on her any minute, I think she might fall apart completely.

I decide to lighten the mood again. "I think we have a much bigger problem, Ma."

She gives me a worried look.

"How am I going to explain to people that I'm the same age as my mother?"

CHAPTER TWENTY-ONE

I t's a couple of hours later, and my mother's gone to stay with her sister in Philly until my situation has been resolved one way or the other.

Not surprisingly, this little family reunion took its toll on all of us emotionally. And, even though most of our evening was spent with my mother and me taking turns comforting each other, I'm keenly aware that Janine is in a world of hurt of her own as she wonders whether she's thrown away her life's work forever.

I peek out the window for the hundredth time, terrified I'll see a fleet of black Genescence sedans turn the corner and finish us off once and for all.

"We can't stay here," Janine says.

"I know. I'm just getting some cash and clothes, and we're gone."

"Can I ask what happened to your father?"

"Train derailment in China. That was seven years ago."

"I'm sorry. I'm lucky. My parents are divorced, but still around."

"Cops, you said, right? Three generations."

"Most of the men, some of the women. Except my mother. She's an architect. She's been living in London with her second husband for the last five years, but we're still close. I have a much younger sister named Emily. Actually, she's my half sister. Very British. Very sweet. I wish I could see her and my mom more often."

"At least they're still around," I say more bitterly than I intend to. "Sorry. As you might have guessed, I didn't handle losing my dad too well. Practically dropped out of school, lost myself in girls and motorcycles and hanging out with guys like Lonny."

"You were just a kid."

"Irony is, lately I was starting to get my act together. Decent job. Even thinking of . . ."

"What?" She moves closer. "Meeting someone? Growing old together?"

"I've already done the growing old part, thank you very much," I say lightly. Then, with a smile, I add, "Anyway, why would I want that? I'm just a kid, remember?"

I head into the kitchen as a lost-in-thought Janine stares into space. I return a minute later with a big bag of pretzels. I put it down on the coffee table.

"For the road. You as hungry as I am?"

Suddenly, Janine smashes her hand down on the bag, sending crushed pretzels flying in every direction.

"I guess not," I deadpan.

Janine stands up, moves around restlessly.

"Know what? I hate TimeLock. I hate Walter. And I hate you."

"Me? What did *I* do? I mean, lately."

Janine stares out the window. "I'm a damn good agent, Morgan. Loyal, hardworking, by the book. I told you I was the first one in my family to join the bureau. All these cops, then I come along and break protocol. And my father gave me shit for it, but finally . . . finally . . . two years ago, he said he was proud of me. And you know what? *I* was proud of me too. Now I've thrown the whole thing away and, worst of all, let down my boss, the man who mentored me from the very beginning."

"Walter's an idiot," I say.

"Walter's doing his job. I broke the law I swore to uphold. I've become reckless, impulsive, and irresponsible."

"Let me guess. This is where I come in."

"Right. But it's not your fault either. It's me. I let my personal feelings compromise my professional integrity."

"Personal feelings about TimeLock? Or about me?"

She doesn't answer, but her demeanor softens a bit. I move toward her gingerly.

A bittersweet smile crosses Janine's face. "Walter's in love with me."

I knew it. I heard the way he spoke to her. I saw the way he looked at her. Not unlike the way I'm looking at her right this minute.

"Can I ask . . .?"

"No. Never. Not my type. Actually, too much my type. Job above all else. One-track mind. Never breaking the rules. It would be like dating myself with male genitalia."

I laugh. "Well, there's an image that'll haunt me for the rest of my life." I move ever so slightly closer to her and say, "Let me guess. You're one of those straightlaced women who can't help but be attracted to the occasional bad boy."

"Fine. You got me. But that was in my twenties. The truth is that three years ago, thirty hit like a ton of bricks, and I figured I'd finally evolved past all that."

"Until I came along."

"Stop making this about you. My life is spinning out of control right now, so let's stick with me, okay?"

"Okay. Listen, Janine, we were both right all along. The program is screwed up. If we don't do this, they win."

She continues to look out the window, then says, "Even if we have to keep breaking the law? That's not how I was raised, Morgan. That's not who I am."

I put my hand on her shoulder. "That's not who you *were*. We all change. *I* did."

She gently puts her hand on my face with a smile. "Seriously—don't you ever shave?"

"Come on, let's see Dr. Garvey." I toss her my mother's car keys. "Back the car out, will you? I'll meet you in front."

I pack some more clothes as Janine moves off toward the garage. I hear my mother's car start up and peer out the window to see it backing out. But as the garage door starts to close, I spot headlights sweeping around the corner: a black sedan! It pulls up behind the car. Shit.

I kill the living room light and look outside as Colby and Tyler emerge from the sedan. Looks like Coombs is behind the wheel. Don't these guys ever take a day off? Colby moves to the car and signals for Janine to lower the window. No? He takes out his gun. She can lower it, or he fires. Janine lowers it. Now Patrick Loder emerges from the back of the sedan, moves to her. I open the window so I can hear as I desperately try to figure out what to do.

"Step out, please," Loder tells Janine, sounding like a highway patrolman. All that's missing is the moustache. Colby opens the door, and a defiant Janine gets out.

"I'm FBI, you stupid son of a bitch. You sure you want to be doing this?"

"Tell him to come out," Loder demands, meaning me, of course.

"He's not here. Just checking on his mother."

"Don't insult my intelligence."

"Screw you."

Colby holds Janine as Loder smacks her. Hard. But she remains silent.

"Morgan! Your girlfriend would like to discuss your plans for the evening."

Another vicious smack.

"Don't do this, Loder," Janine says.

"It doesn't matter what I do, Agent Price. I don't expect your cooperation."

He exposes Janine's neck. Colby moves in with a switchblade and opens it with a *click*!

I have no choice, so I head into the garage, push a button, and raise the door. Loder and his thugs look over, welcoming my apparent surrender. What they don't know is what I've kept in this garage all these years: an old motorcycle I bought as a teenager to retrofit but promised my mother I'd never ride—a promise I actually kept. I also spot some sporting equipment, including a baseball bat.

I rig the ignition, fire up the bike, and race toward Colby, cracking his head with the bat as Janine punches the distracted Tyler in the face and sends him flying. Meanwhile, I skid into a one-eighty and roar back toward Loder, who has to dive to avoid both the motorcycle and the swinging bat.

Coombs pops out of the sedan, heading for Janine. She crunches his nose with a palm, knees him savagely. Meanwhile, Tyler groggily rises and fumbles for his dropped gun. But I zoom by and crack the bat across his knees. Tyler goes down, and his gun goes flying as

Colby shakes off cobwebs and attacks Janine with a right cross that sends her reeling. She picks up a loose brick, hurls it, and knocks Colby down on his knees even as I spin around, zip past with the swinging bat, and knock him all the way to the ground.

Coombs fires, but wildly, panicking now that the odds have changed. He starts to run, but I catch up and again swing the bat. Coombs hits the driveway.

Meanwhile, Loder retreats to the sedan, opens the door. Janine slams it on his fingers. Loder bellows. I jump off the bike, whirl Loder around, and punch him in the stomach. Then again. And again. Blood sputters from Loder's mouth.

"Enough," shouts Janine.

The lights of a fast-approaching car blanket the scene. What a shock, it's another black sedan. Time to leave. Janine scoops up a dropped gun, jumps into the passenger seat of my mother's car as I climb behind the wheel.

"Go!" yells Janine, and we speed off.

CHAPTER TWENTY-TWO

We're about to either do something very wise or incredibly stupid—and, based on some of my recent moves, stupid might be a safe bet. Dr. Lionel Garvey has always been a giant question mark in all of this. Is he some mad genius pulling the strings in the background, a pawn in Loder's evil plot, or another innocent caught in Genescence's deadly cover-up?

One thing about Dr. Garvey is certain, however. This is the man who created TimeLock—and for that, I can never forgive him.

"Shouldn't you be calling the FBI or the police?" I ask Janine as we speed toward Garvey's house. "You saw what Loder and his hit squad are capable of. I promise I won't run."

"I will when we have more. Turn right at the next corner."

We're now in a posh neighborhood of Washington replete with stately, upscale homes. We stop before a red-brick Georgian. A light rain is falling. I ring the bell.

"Yes?" A woman's voice comes through an intercom.

"My name's Morgan Eberly. I've got to see Dr. Garvey."

"I'm afraid that's impossible."

"Tell him I was in the second processing group."

We hear voices raised inside, then the door finally opens. Anna Warner is there, with Dr. Garvey behind her.

Janine introduces herself, and we're escorted into Garvey's study.

"Close the door please, Anna," Dr. Garvey says. She does so and moves toward his side. Their relationship is unclear, but I can sense that a powerful bond of trust exists between them.

"Eberly?" Garvey says quietly. Then his eyes open wide in stunned recognition and he adds, "You're one of the three . . ."

"Who escaped. I got lucky—if you can call any of this luck. You know what's going on, don't you?"

Garvey looks troubled, but says nothing.

"Everything's crazy. They're killing people. Do you know that?"

"Killing people? What are you talking about?"

"Two of the men who escaped that day are dead. Loder's men have tried to kill us several times, and they must have knocked off a dozen or so from the first group. How can you not know all that?"

"That's insane! That's impossible!" a stunned Garvey says.

"It's true, Dr. Garvey," Janine chimes in. She shows her ID, in this case an FBI parking pass since she turned over her badge to Walter.

Though Dr. Garvey doesn't question the absence of a proper badge, Janine offers an explanation anyway, clearly hoping her own candor might inspire the doctor to be straightforward with us. "Truth is," she continues, "the FBI and I are on a little break, what with my harboring an escaped convict and all. But you have to believe us. Loder's been systematically wiping out TimeLock prisoners from Loomis since the get-go. Some of them looked like accidents or suicides, but they were all murders. And they all had one thing in common: the bodies were either burned or never found."

Enough politeness. I go hard at Garvey: "And you know exactly why, don't you, 'Doctor?'"

Garvey looks down.

"Something went wrong, didn't it? Some of the guys started to get a little old before their time, right?"

"Just one that I know of . . ."

"Lonny. Lawrence Myers?"

"Yes! That was his name! Poor Lawrence. He . . . metamorphosed, I suppose would be the best word . . . a short time after his group was processed. It didn't kill him, but it would have soon enough. Suddenly, we knew. We desperately tried to find Mr. Myers, but no luck. I ran tests. It turned out to be the mix of kalopheen, the mineral compound that's central to the process. But it was too late for the first two groups, and Loder swore to me . . . he swore to God!"

"God?" I say. "I don't think Loder and God have been in touch for quite a while. What did he swear?"

"That they would all be contacted, brought in, the minute I could formulate an antitoxin."

"Did you?"

"I'm not sure yet."

I jump in: "But Loder couldn't take a chance. All those guys out there were walking billboards for a billion-dollar program that doesn't work. Including one of the men who escaped with me from Loomis who aged from fifty to infinity right in front of us just this morning."

Garvey takes a long breath; his look is distant, his voice a soft-flowing river of remorse. Anna squeezes his arm. Garvey is silent for a moment, then quietly says, "When people like Loder come along, they sweep away everything before them, especially people like me. We are the unwitting adjuncts of these great movers and shakers. There were rumors about Loder's past, but I chose to ignore them. Colorful rumors involving the arms trade, money laundering, and drug-running before he settled down, so to speak, by purchasing a high-tech pharmaceutical company which he named Genescence. And that's when I met him . . ." He gestures toward Anna. "When *we* met him. Our 'savior.'"

"Please, Lionel!" Anna implores.

"So that's where his goons come from," Janine says. "From Loder's good old days." Then her eyes open wide. "What about Morgan? Doesn't he need this antitoxin?"

"I really don't know," Garvey says. "It's in my lab at Genescence, but it's under heavy guard. I have some here, but I haven't been able to test its efficacy yet."

"Maybe Morgan should take it now while he can," Janine offers.

"That could be dangerous," Garvey says. "It would only work once someone is symptomatic. Extreme weakness, dizziness, headaches. Have you experienced any of those symptoms, Morgan?"

I shake my head.

"Good. The problem is that taking the antitoxin before symptoms develop could be fatal. And the untested batch I have here could be especially deadly, I'm afraid."

"In other words, I might be a goner either way," I say.

"No! Not everyone who was processed had an adverse reaction. You may well be one of the lucky ones. In fact, time is on your side now."

Garvey pauses, then adds, "Time. There's the irony. I never set out to accelerate aging. Who would do such a thing? I was looking for the Fountain of Youth."

"Only it didn't work out that way," I say, stating the obvious.

"Loder was ready to pull the plug, but he got a reprieve of sorts. Myra Winters."

"In a country devastated by rampant crime and prison overcrowding, Loder and Governor Winters saw the potential of TimeLock," Janine says, "and you were back in business."

"A business I found unholy from the start. But I had no choice . . ."

Garvey and Anna exchange meaningful looks. I'm tempted to ask why he had no choice, but this isn't the time to go tripping down memory lane.

Which is precisely why Janine cuts to the chase and asks the question that will settle once and for all in our minds what Dr. Garvey's level of culpability really is.

"Will you talk to the authorities?"

"Yes, if it helps," he says unhesitatingly. "But there may be a credibility problem."

"Between you and Loder? Who would take his word over yours?"

"There are powerful lobbies working for TimeLock. People in government like Myra Winters, who may well become the next president of the United States. In great part *because* of this program. People so enamored of TimeLock that any hint of a problem becomes heresy. And there is, quite frankly, the problem of personal survival. I will not put my wife in danger, Mr. Eberly."

So they *are* married. An unlikely couple, but then again, so are Janine and I. If, that is, we ever become one.

"Loder will do everything he can to silence me now," Dr. Garvey says.

"I can help with protection," Janine says.

And I add, "Isn't there something in writing? Some kind of paper trail?"

"Yes, I was coming to that. The documentation we need is in my office."

"Where?" I ask.

"Computer file."

"Wouldn't Loder know about it?"

"Yes, and I'm sure he'll hunt it down and destroy it. But there's also a well-concealed backup file."

"Can I get to it from the outside?"

"Impossible."

Janine points to me. "He broke into the FBI and the FAA, Dr. Garvey. Don't be so sure."

I say, "At the risk of being immodest, Dr. Garvey, I have a little experience in that area."

"This isn't a matter of bypassing a firewall, Mr. Eberly. Access depends entirely on being there and having the right key card."

Call it ageism, but I'm more than a little surprised a man pushing sixty-five knows anything about firewalls.

Then again, I'm still doing life-and-death motorcycle stunts and I'm almost forty-five.

"Then we've got to go for it," I tell Garvey. "The only question is when?"

"Tonight's impossible. They'd wonder why I'm there, and it might draw too much attention."

"You have that morning meeting in New York tomorrow," Anna says. "I could take you to the office first."

"Yes, that would work," Garvey says. Then he turns to Janine and me and says, "Where are you staying? You've got to get out of sight."

"Perhaps here?" Anna says.

Janine shakes her head. "Thank you, but that's clustering the target. And my place is out."

"Can't you go to the FBI?" Garvey asks.

"Not now. Like I said, I'm kind of on the run myself."

"The River Inn!" says Anna. "It's secluded and very private."

"I know it. Good idea," says Janine. "But not under either of our names, of course."

"Of course," Anna says. "Under the name Garrett." Once again, she and Garvey exchange glances. Does the name Garrett have some special meaning to them?

Anna moves to a phone to make a reservation, and Garvey says, "We'll regroup in the morning."

"Here's my cell," Janine says as she hands Dr. Garvey a card.

"Stay safe," he says.

"Thank you, Dr. Garvey," Janine responds. "At the slightest sign of trouble, you call Walter Greene at the FBI. Or the police. Or me."

CHAPTER
TWENTY-THREE

Given its name, we expected the River Inn to be situated alongside a river. What we didn't expect is how utterly charming it is. Not to mention quiet and secluded. Just what we need right now.

When Anna made the reservation, we never thought to tell her to get two separate rooms, and that's fine with me. Not for romantic reasons, but because we're safer together at this point. Plus I'd really rather not be alone right now.

If I *were* romantically inclined tonight, however, this would be the perfect setting. The room drips colonial hospitality. Copper and wood everywhere. A crackling fire. Outside, rain splatters the windows. All that's missing is a violinist.

"Wow," says Janine.

"I thought you were going to say, 'What am I doing here?'"

"That's what I meant. Wow, what am I doing here?"

I smile and run my fingers along her neck.

"And what do you think you're doing?" Janine asks as if she doesn't know the answer.

"Want me to stop?"

"Well . . . yes . . . maybe. I need time . . . I need toothpaste."

She pulls free and goes into the bathroom. I open the French windows, move onto a balcony and into the drizzle. I turn my face into it, and it feels good, liberating. I hear a sound and turn around to see Janine come out of the bathroom wearing a sweater and nothing else. She gets under the covers.

I reenter the room, take off my shirt and everything else, and slither under the covers.

"You're soaked," Janine says.

"Still wondering?" I ask.

"You mean, what am I doing here?"

I nod. "You could have asked for two rooms twenty minutes ago."

"I could have. Absolutely."

"Because you don't need this."

"I do not."

"And, let's face it, once you've put this rogue agent phase behind you, you'll be ready to rejoin your smooth-as-silk Walter Greene life instead of hiding from a bunch of thugs who are trying to blow you away or spending the night with a guy you wouldn't normally think twice about, let alone be in bed with."

"Yup, that about covers it."

"Especially if you look at it on paper. Nothing in common. I mean zilch."

"Less than zilch."

"But here we are. And then there's the question of complicating your life."

"Not a problem."

"Because I'll never mean that much to you."

"I'm starting to forget about you already."

"Come here."

"And why would I do that?"

"Because you can't help yourself."

"That's what worries me."

She smiles and moves into my arms.

CHAPTER TWENTY-FOUR

Early morning. The sun is out. Birds noisily chirp. Janine and I are wrapped around each other, sound asleep. Her long hair covers both of our faces.

Suddenly, we're jolted awake by several loud thumps at the door. And this from the hallway: "Police! We have an arrest warrant for Morgan Eberly! Open up!"

Janine bounds to the door, looks through the peephole, mouths: "They're for real!" How in the world did they find us? Janine hastens over, wrapping a sheet around herself.

"Stall them," I say.

"Great. More to add to my rap sheet."

I slip on some clothes as Janine drapes the sheet more seductively around her and moves to the door.

She opens it, leaving the chain on, and says in her best floozie voice, "What's up, Officer?"

"Open the door now!"

"Hey, give us a break! We're right in the middle, okay?" She smiles a cheap smile and accidentally drops the sheet. "Oops!"

I open the French windows and climb down the side of the building as Janine covers herself and opens the door to find two cops ogling her.

Seconds later, I'm running across the grounds toward the river. I look back and see the two cops climbing down from our room and giving chase. I make my way along a gravel path and breathe a sigh of relief. This was easier than I thought. Which is exactly when I find myself running right toward two more officers.

I veer off and bolt down another pathway alongside the river. The cops are in pursuit, and one of them shouts, "Stop right there!" Thanks for the offer, but I don't think so.

I race into a building and find myself in a huge open-air market and food court where merchants are unloading early-morning deliveries and preparing to open their shops. The cops are fast approaching and in far better shape than I am, so I grab a baseball cap from one of the just-opened stores, and try to look inconspicuous. After lingering near the store for what seems like an eternity with the two cops still close by looking for me, I start to walk off toward the exit. And, suddenly, I become very conspicuous because the store owner is yelling at me: "Hey, you didn't pay for the cap!"

This draws the attention of the cops, so I toss the cap back to the owner and run toward the exit. In an alleyway behind a street full of shops and restaurants, I decide to go through the back door of a bakery, turning around for a second to see only one of the policemen still in pursuit.

I burst into the bakery and promptly find myself crashing right into the second cop. His partner rushes in as I'm being handcuffed, and then the two officers push me toward the back door. Looking ahead to my imminent return to the slammer, an odd thought crosses my mind as I'm being taken away past the bakery's heavenly-scented ovens: I hope they deliver.

An hour later, I'm at a police station about to be transported back to my old stomping ground, Loomis Detention Center. It was a one-in-a-million fluke that freed me from there in the first place, so I guess it was inevitable that my adventure with TimeLock would come full circle.

A guard gruffly leads me to a cell, and the door clangs shut.

"Who'd you knock off this time?" the guard says.

"They haven't told me yet," I answer truthfully. But I can guess—Loder's behind my arrest. He must have had Dr. Garvey's phone tapped, figured out that Anna's reservation at the River Inn might actually have been for us, then told the cops where to find the famous escapee from TimeLock.

Unless, of course, Garvey turned me in himself.

Either way, it's a sure bet that the bad guys want me silenced for good, and I'm not long for this world.

CHAPTER TWENTY-FIVE

Behind the police station, I'm escorted out by a guard. I guess it's time to head back to Club Loomis. I spot Janine in the driver's seat of my mom's car, which fills me with boundless relief. She's wearing dark sunglasses and a black suit jacket—completely looking the part of an FBI agent. And then I see a black sedan pulling into the parking lot, which fills me with abject terror. But the sedan pulls back out to the main road.

When the sedan is out of sight, Janine lowers her window, authoritatively says "FBI" to the guard and flashes what he will hopefully assume is some kind of agency ID, but which I know is in fact her Costco membership card. Fortunately, she's commanding enough to pull off the deception.

"Just throw him in the back," Janine instructs the guard. Sure enough, he shoves me—still handcuffed—into the back seat like a sack of potatoes. Janine nods a curt thank-you to the guard, and the car shoots off.

Suddenly, Janine hits the brakes hard. Is the black sedan closing in? Would they be stupid enough to make a move on us behind a police station? Apparently not. Janine backs the car up to where the guard is still standing.

"Keys," she says, and the guard hands her the handcuff keys. In the same second, a sergeant comes running out of the building, waving his hands and shouting, "Hold it!"

Clearly, the cops are on to us. But Janine hits the gas, and we rush off. She then holds out the keys, and I take them in my teeth. With the car twisting and turning, I drop them several times, but finally unlock the cuffs.

"Cops on our tail?" I ask.

"Not yet."

I look back, and there's a familiar black sedan in pursuit with two men I don't recognize inside.

"We've got company!" I shout, then add with a nervous smile, "I've always wanted to say that!"

Janine's cell phone rings. She's trying to keep us from driving off the road, so she tosses it to me.

"My friend Sergeant Mason back at the station, I'm guessing," says Janine. "I convinced him I'd been assigned to take you back to Loomis."

But it's not Sergeant Mason. It's Anna.

"Anna, it's Morgan."

"Something's wrong, Morgan. Lionel went to his office this morning—just the way we planned—but he didn't come out. Loder and his men took off with him in the company helicopter, supposedly heading to the airport, then on to New York. There's no way Lionel would be keeping that meeting voluntarily."

"Loder knows you both helped us, so you're right— he's being forced to go. Where do they fly out of?"

She gives me the name and address of the private airport. I tell Janine, and we speed off.

Ten minutes later, we approach the small airport's outer perimeter. There are a few corporate jets and a dozen or so small planes. The only good news is that Janine appears to have lost the goons chasing us.

"Look!" Janine shouts. I follow her gaze and spot the Genescence jet taxiing toward the warm-up circle for takeoff.

"Morgan, switch. You'd better drive!"

Good idea. Janine is the marksman. With the car still moving, I awkwardly move myself to the front passenger seat, then we switch places. Janine takes out her gun.

I turn onto a narrow dirt road that runs toward the runway. The fence around the field is about six feet high. I head for a pile of dumped dirt that creates a shallow ramp, flooring it.

"What are you doing?" Janine shouts.

"Going in the back way, where they can't see us coming."

I roar up the "ramp," and we go soaring, barely clearing the fence and smacking down onto a dirt field.

"Lot easier on a bike," I mutter as Janine glares at me.

We see the jet slowly turning, preparing for takeoff. I step on the gas to try to intercept it, and, seconds later, the jet starts its run. This is going to be close. The plane is about to hit its stride.

I angle the car, and we shoot across the nose of the jet long enough for the pilot to swerve, then kill the power and hit the brakes. The plane skids, coming to a stop in the grass off the runway.

A second later, the passenger door slides up, and stairs automatically descend. We spot Garvey desperately trying to escape as Colby and Tyler rush after him.

I skid to a stop, and Janine starts firing on the emerging Tyler. As she does so, Garvey is able to get away, and he climbs into the back seat.

Tyler races toward us, his gun spitting out a barrage of bullets. But Janine squeezes off two shots, and Tyler goes sprawling, dead. I get out of the car and make a run for Tyler's gun just as Colby appears in the doorway of the jet.

Janine doesn't see him, and she's now an easy target. I take aim and pull the trigger. Colby is flung back—a shoulder crease, but damaging enough to force him to drop the gun. He retreats into the safety of the fuselage as Janine and I climb back into the car, me behind the wheel once again. We roar off just as Loder steps out of the plane and slams his hand against the fuselage in fury.

CHAPTER TWENTY-SIX

Garvey is on his cell. "Anna! Yes, yes, I'm fine. Where are you? Stay there. We're on the way—fifteen minutes. Bye."

He puts down the phone. "She's at the mall. Tyson's Corner. Agent Price, what exactly are you planning? You can't go in alone. You need help."

Janine turns to me. "He's right, Morgan."

I nod. Anything's better than mixing it up again with Loder and company.

Janine pulls out her cell, punches a button. She fills Walter Greene in on our latest adventures, and we can hear his booming voice throughout the car. He is not amused.

"I can't believe you, Janine! You expect me to forward this . . . preposterous idea upstairs? With a personal endorsement? We'd need court orders, procedural approval. You're on suspension, and this whole thing is highly irregular!"

Seeing Janine's infuriated reaction, I grab the phone.

"Walter, we've got a big-time emergency here! You don't want J. Edgar to turn over in his dress, do you?"

Janine grabs the phone back. "Damn it, Morgan, that's not going to help!"

"Maybe this will," Garvey says as he gestures for the phone. Janine hands it over as Garvey whispers to her, "Who are we talking to?"

"Walter Greene," Janine responds.

"Agent Greene, this is Dr. Lionel Garvey. Everything you've heard is true. Something has got to be done about Patrick Loder and TimeLock, and it has to be done now!"

Given Dr. Garvey's global reputation, it's more than likely that Walter is duly impressed, maybe even convinced. Unfortunately, however, Walter responds with this: "Sir, I don't have the authority to initiate something like this without the proper sanction."

Garvey shakes his head, and Janine takes the phone back from him.

"Walter, we're under attack out here. At least let us come in, and we can discuss the proper sanction later."

"Of course. I'll start the paperwork."

Janine rolls her eyes and hangs up.

"What a wuss," says Garvey, and Janine and I exchange amused glances. *Wuss* is hardly a word we'd expect from a sixty-five-year-old Nobel finalist, but at this point, nothing should surprise us anymore.

"Obviously, we need that file," Janine says.

Janine turns to Garvey. "Don't worry, Dr. Garvey. You and Anna will be safe. But Morgan and I have to do this now. If we turn ourselves in, we may never have the chance to nail Loder again."

"Two problems," I say. "First one is getting in. You could help, Doc."

"His ID!" says Janine. Then to Garvey: "What do you think?

"It's yours, of course. But how do you deal with the problem of Loder? He probably went back to Genescence to wait for your next move."

Janine thinks for a moment. "Then we have to make sure our next move is a complete surprise."

"How so?"

"By playing it straight and talking to him. I go through the lobby, ask to meet with him. He obviously knows who I am. He'll wonder what it's all about. He'll see me."

"Are you nuts?" I say. "First of all, he probably knows you're suspended."

"I'm not going there to arrest him, just trying to reason with him."

"Which leads to my 'second of all'—he's a fucking lunatic!"

"That probably should have been your 'first of all.'"

I'm not smiling.

"Fine," she says. "It's crazy, but it's all we've got. I'll distract him. He can't be sure I don't have twenty agents waiting to swoop in. While he's trying to piece everything together, you access the file in Dr. Garvey's office."

"Right, then Colby shoots us both, and it's game over."

No reaction from Janine.

"But we're doing it anyway."

"Yup."

I shake my head. We're going for a Hail Mary, and we don't even have possession of the football.

"You do have one advantage," Garvey says. "Tonight's the big event. The president and Myra Winters are announcing that TimeLock is about to go national."

Janine responds, "Which means Loder wouldn't dare go after me—at least not today."

"Oh, really?" I say sarcastically. "Are you forgetting how they tried to knock me off when I crashed their last big soiree?"

"No choice, Morgan. We're playing it my way. Though getting in with so many cops and Secret Service guarding the place won't be easy."

"I'm betting your Costco card won't do the trick this time."

"Don't worry, I'll get in somehow."

Knowing Janine, I don't doubt it for a second.

I pull the car off the road and stop. Garvey fishes his ID out of his wallet, hands it over, then quickly sketches a diagram.

"Shortcut to my office—follow the arrows. The file name is Ponce de Leon." A smile. "I couldn't help myself."

He scribbles some numbers. "Here's the access code. After you punch it in, the system will ask to scan your ID—my ID. Save the file to a memory stick—they're on my desk—and then, as if I need to remind you, both of you get out as fast as you can!"

Janine and I exchange nervous glances. I think we'll remember.

A few minutes later, we roll up alongside Garvey's car at Tyson's Corner. Anna jumps out as Garvey does the same. They embrace as if they haven't seen each other for years. It's kinda sweet, actually.

"Are you all right?" Anna asks.

"Yes, of course. Just one second." He moves toward my side of the car and peers in.

"Thank you. Take care of yourselves."

"You too," Janine and I say simultaneously.

Janine hands Garvey a card. "Walter Greene is expecting you at this address. It's close by, but I can have him send a car to pick you up."

"This is less than five miles from here. We'll be fine. Thank you again."

Now Garvey takes a look at me, the first time he's really seen me clearly after being in the back seat this whole time.

"How do you feel, Morgan?" he asks, and I suddenly have a giant lump in my throat.

In a playful voice that sounds as forced as it is, I say, "Pretty good, Doc. How about you?"

"I don't like your skin tone. Recovery entails a critical crossover period. You should be days past it, but now I can't be sure."

"I'm good, Doc. We're wasting time."

"What is it?" Janine asks Garvey nervously.

I'm not sure I want to hear the answer.

"Probably nothing, but just in case symptoms suddenly develop, I'd feel better if you have some of the antitoxin I've developed on hand. The lab at Genescence will be sealed tight as a drum, so my home lab is the best option right now. Damn. I should have given it to you when you were there. I was afraid it might cause . . ." His voice trails off.

"Don't blame yourself, Dr. Garvey. I appreciate the concern, but we don't have time for me to play guinea pig."

Janine forcefully interrupts. "What are you trying to do? Sacrifice yourself? You saw what happened to Rajek. That could be you, Morgan!"

"We haven't got time for another experiment! The antidote might work, or it might not. I might need it, and I might not. Listen, I'm not being noble, my money's on the file, so let's find it!"

"No," Garvey says forcefully. "Stopping at our house will take only a few minutes, and it could save your life. I'll go with you."

"Absolutely not," I insist. "We can't risk losing you."

Janine interjects, "I'll get backup."

I mull it over, then finally say, "Fine, I'll go."

"Good," Garvey says as he hands me a set of keys. "Big key'll get you in the front or back door. Security code is Kiyoko25. That's k-i-y-o-k-o-2-5. The lab is in the cellar. Go to the refrigerator and look for a vial labeled GS75. One vial is all you'll need. Swallow the whole thing, but only—and I can't stress this enough—*only* if you start to feel faint and shaky, and if your vision gets blurry. Otherwise, don't go near it. I'll check you out later. Now, go!"

"Thank you, Doctor. Stay safe," I say to Garvey and Anna as I back out of the parking space, then speed toward the highway.

CHAPTER
TWENTY-SEVEN

We drive up to Garvey's house a few minutes later, and a couple of FBI agents get out of their car and wave. Janine obviously recognizes them, and she gestures for the two agents to follow us as we make our way toward the front door.

Just then, however, a Genescence sedan speeds onto Garvey's street, and a series of shots are fired from within. With the window lowered, I can see two men I vaguely recognize from my visit to Genescence, one behind the wheel and the other in the passenger seat firing a semiautomatic rifle. The two FBI guys, Janine, and I scramble to safety on the side on the house, and the agents return fire. The driver swerves the car around, and more shots are fired, but there's no way they can get to us, so he speeds off.

Janine gestures, and the two agents race to their car, get in, and take off in pursuit. Janine calls the incident in to her office and requests additional backup.

"Let's get out of here!" I tell Janine, but she shakes her head.

"Not till we have what we came for."

I nod reluctantly, and we continue around the back of the house and enter through the rear door. Once the alarm system has been shut off, we hurry toward the stairs to the cellar and head down into Dr. Garvey's lab. I open the refrigerator, find one of the vials, and put it in my pocket. We both freeze as we hear more screeching tires coming from the front of the house. We hurry upstairs and look out the window to see a bandaged Colby and a man I don't recognize getting out of—what else?—a black sedan. My God, don't these people know cars come in other colors? Guns drawn, they run toward the front door and shoot their way in.

Janine takes out her gun and fires, instantly killing the second man. Colby scurries behind a sofa and fires several shots our way, barely missing Janine. I dive for cover and feel a sharp pain in my side. At first, I think I've been shot, and a wave of panic washes over me. But the pain is minor, and there's no blood, which is when I realize that I wasn't shot at all. Instead, I crushed the vial of antitoxin when I dove for cover.

Not seeing any of this, Janine gestures toward the back door. We need to get out of here. Dodging more bullets, we run out the back door, climb over a fence into a neighbor's backyard, then emerge on the street and jump into our car. I speed off as we spot Colby emerging from the front of the house and climbing into the sedan.

Janine again calls the bureau, and is told a team of agents, along with the police, will be on the scene shortly. I'm sorry the vial didn't survive the ordeal, but I thank God we did.

CHAPTER
TWENTY-EIGHT

Our car is approaching the Potomac as we spot a police chopper whizzing overhead. Did Walter put out an APB on us? How would he know what vehicle we'd be in?

In any case, the chopper passes overhead, and we take a deep breath.

Unfortunately, however, our relief is short-lived. The police helicopter has no interest in us and is soon gone, but, seconds later, the roar of an engine fills the air. It's another chopper. This time, it's Genescence's black (of course) two-engine attack helicopter. It makes a low pass, Uzi spurting.

Our back window is blown away, and I hit the pedal, speeding over the Key Bridge. The chopper arcs around. An eighteen-wheeler's just ahead. I dart into the protection afforded by the truck's right side, and the helicopter soars overhead, then whips around again. I brake sharply, then zip ahead along the truck's left side. In the cab of the eighteen-wheeler, the driver is fuming. What am I doing? In our car, Janine is also fuming. The sudden turns and stops have sent her much-needed cell phone flying out the window.

The attack copter angles and bears down on us from straight ahead, weapon on autofire. Again, I stomp on the brakes, then swing in to tailgate the big truck.

We race off the bridge and onto the Whitehurst Freeway in lockstep with the truck. Not surprisingly, the truck swerves toward the first available off-ramp. As does every other vehicle in sight that finds itself in the middle of this sudden demolition derby.

For a moment, there is blessed quiet. Janine and I look around. Where's the chopper? I turn onto Virginia Avenue and speed past the Watergate.

"Maybe we lost them," Janine says optimistically.

Yeah, sure. Here he comes now out of nowhere. Bullets fly. There's a pickup truck ahead of our car with two teenagers inside it. Their windshield disintegrates, and the hood dots up like Swiss cheese. The steering's shot. The pickup weaves crazily, forcing us into the side of a van. Luckily, the two teens pull over to safety as Janine and I abandon our car. We race down Virginia Avenue and head for the Lincoln Memorial. The Genescence chopper roars in again, this time unbelievably low, the exact height of a tour bus that looms ahead.

Finally, we hear sirens headed our way, but even that doesn't seem to dissuade the helicopter from gunning after us. Fortunately, this is the heart of Washington—the ultimate no-fly zone—so we're beyond relieved when military jets and helicopters soar into view to go after our pursuers. Janine and I race toward the Lincoln Memorial. I become acutely aware once again that I'm running as a forty-three-year-old man now and not a twenty-three-year-old kid. I gesture to Janine to go on without me, but she'll have none of it. She tugs on my arm, and I huff and puff behind her.

As the sirens approach and we see jets and choppers dotting the sky and heading toward the action, we enter the sanctum of the memorial. Close enough to climb onto Lincoln's lap, we're safe now. It doesn't last long.

The black chopper inches around the side of the Lincoln Memorial like some enormous insect crawling around the building at the same level as the Great Emancipator himself. The engine's thunderous roar reverberates throughout the chamber, and visitors scramble in all directions.

You want gutsy? The chopper keeps on coming into the gaping maw of the chamber—actually inside! At the partially open door, Coombs can be seen with the Uzi, a guy I don't recognize alongside him. He aims, a fish-in-the-barrel shot. But now the pilot's waving frantically, pointing to the army helicopters and jets streaking in.

The Genescence chopper swivels like a top, inches back out, whines into a full-power climb, and veers up and away. The military jets and chopper are in hot pursuit, but they're not about to down their target in the middle of the city. Once the black helicopter clears the area and is above a large empty field, however, one of the military choppers unloads a barrage of gunfire, and the Genescence helicopter explodes in a spectacular fireball.

As all this is going down, the first of many police cars zips up. We rush toward it. Janine reaches for her badge, again forgetting she doesn't have it anymore.

"It's okay. We know who you are. Your boss sent out the alert. Sergeant Cassandra Abernathy at your service."

"Sergeant, we need help!" I say needlessly.

"You think?" the sergeant says with a warm smile.

"Sergeant Abernathy, we know who's behind all this. Can you take us to Genescence in Silver Springs?" Janine asks.

The sergeant nods, and we pile into the car and speed off.

CHAPTER TWENTY-NINE

The last time I was here, I barely escaped with my life on Lonny's motorcycle. This time, we're entering the Genescence facility in a police car. Why am I still trembling?

Sergeant Abernathy parks as close as she can to the entrance. Which isn't all that close, because the scene is bedlam. Dozens of vehicles and Secret Service agents dot the landscape. Media trucks are everywhere. Tonight's the big night.

"Sorry, I can't get you any closer," the sergeant says.

"This is great. Thanks, Sergeant," I tell her.

"You sure you don't want me to come in?"

"Just be close by if this goes south."

"President's coming later, so I'm not going anywhere."

"Every time I'm here, they're throwing a party," I comment.

"Like I said," Janine says, "even Loder wouldn't do anything reckless with Bartlett here."

"Yeah, he's well known for his restraint."

"I think I can stall Loder for ten minutes tops," Janine says. "Hopefully, that'll give you enough time to get the file from Garvey's computer."

"I'll do it in five," I say with a smile that quickly vanishes as I add, "I still don't like this, Janine. We've got Walter on our side now, not to mention that a Genescence chopper just chased us through half of DC."

"Loder will say his men went rogue. Plus it still doesn't tie TimeLock in with the murders. No, it's Trojan horse time."

I nod reluctantly. One thing I've learned by now is not to challenge Janine when it comes to . . . well, anything. Truth be told, she's far braver than I'll ever be, and I've never admired her more.

"Listen—" Janine says warmly.

"I know."

"You know what?"

"Now that you've found me, you don't want to lose me. You never thought you could feel this way about anybody. What we have could never be replaced."

"Just watch your ass," she says.

"That works too."

I give her a perfunctory kiss. We have work to do, and we head off in different directions.

A few minutes later, I move into the south entrance. With security exceptionally tight, I make my way toward the lobby. As before, it's decorated with tables in preparation for the night's grand festivities. I grab a few helpings of shrimp as I pass through.

I'll say this for Genescence: except for all the killing, they sure know how to throw a party.

At the far end of the lobby, I insert Garvey's ID in a slot. Squares of light flash in a sequence of colors. One after another, each square of light goes to green, then a heavy door slides open.

I've made it to the research building where the executive offices are. Consulting Garvey's sketch, I turn onto a new corridor. I check a few office doors, then find Garvey's. I'm about to use the ID again to open his office when a woman appears. Like a female Colby, she's big, tall, and mean-looking.

I hastily pocket the ID and rap on the door.

"Dr. Garvey's at a meeting in New York, and his secretary is working the party," Big, Tall, and Mean says.

"Oh. Thank you," I say nervously. Finally, she disappears. I insert the ID and enter the office. I activate the computer and a screensaver on Garvey's monitor appears—the doctor and Anna, big smiles on their faces. Obviously not taken today.

After inserting Garvey's key card, I type in a few prompts, and a file marked CONFIDENTIAL appears. I deploy a few of my tech tricks to bypass a series of firewalls, open the Ponce De Leon folder, insert a memory stick and pocket it when the files have loaded.

So far, so good. Until a few seconds later, when Loder enters the office, gun in hand. "My goodness. You do get around, Morgan."

He gestures, and I hand over the stick.

"Wonderful! I knew the old bastard was hiding a backup!"

Loder shoves the memory stick in his jacket pocket.

"Tell you what we'll do: we'll take the private elevator down to your new permanent home."

"Where is she?"

"Oh, your girlfriend. Let's just say her little plan backfired. She offered to pull back on the investigation if I would only—how did she put it?—behave myself. Said she would do anything to keep you safe. Very touching. And very foolish."

"I said, where *is* she, Loder?"

"Don't worry. You'll be reunited soon enough."

We head for the elevator, which is alongside a stairway. At the last second, I whirl and shove Loder, who tumbles back over a chair. I start down the stairs. For some reason, Loder doesn't follow me, which should be a relief, but somehow isn't.

At the bottom of the stairs, I rush out to find I'm in a huge control center—the futuristic hub of Genescence.

A half floor above the main control room is a semi-circular balcony. And directly ahead is the capsule production line where several dozen workers are plugging away.

I'm about to head toward the less populated balcony when Loder steps out of the private elevator holding a gun. He points it at me and starts firing. I duck behind some equipment near an experimental vertical chamber, but it's only a matter of seconds until he corners me.

The shooting sends the workers scrambling in all directions.

"What do you think, Morgan? Agent Price to the rescue?"

Despite my likely imminent demise, all I can think about is Janine. Did Loder already dispose of her?

From my pathetic little hiding space behind some equipment, I see the elevator has arrived again. The doors start to open.

"Janine! Look out!" I yell, and Loder turns to see her. Except the elevator is empty. With Loder momentarily distracted, I do a dive and roll, trying to knock Loder down. He sees me and fires, slugs hitting high-voltage machinery. Wires start sizzling and sparking.

Janine appears, but from the stairwell, not the elevator. Ruse accomplished. She points her gun at Loder.

"Do not move precipitously, or you may be shot." Same thing she said to me after Lonny. It isn't exactly "Make my day," but right now it's the best catchphrase I've ever heard.

Loder thinks about it. Finally, he drops his gun. I emerge from hiding.

I move toward Loder. "Let's have it." Meaning, of course, the memory stick. He hesitates.

Janine points the pistol toward Loder's midsection and says, "Right now, or I put a bullet in your balls!"

Now *that's* a catchphrase!

Loder hands over the memory stick but just then, the very same big, tall, and mean-looking female guard emerges from a hallway door holding an automatic weapon.

"Put it down!" she commands Janine.

Instead, Janine spins and fires, and the woman collapses on the floor. But, at the same time, Colby appears on the balcony firing his big-bore revolver. Janine dives for me, pushing me out of the line of fire to safety behind a mainframe. She's hurt, blood staining her shoulder. The gun drops from her fingers.

I pick up her gun and kick-slide out, firing as I do. Colby is hit, and rocks back, and then, on reverse momentum, plunges over the balcony railing and crashes in spread-eagled stillness onto the floor below.

Still on the ground, I turn toward Loder and fire, but the gun is empty. Loder quickly moves toward me, then smirks as I continue squeezing the trigger to no avail. More than that, he can tell my coordination is suddenly diminishing. I can't even point the gun at him, and he smiles with the realization that my body is deteriorating rapidly.

An injured Janine looks on in horror. She saw what happened to Rajek, and now it's about to happen to me. To both of them, I must look like one of those inflatable tube-man balloons you see outside of car dealerships, arms fluttering, legs flopping. Helpfully, Loder takes an arm.

"What a shame, Morgan. I'm afraid TimeLock's caught up with you after all, poor fellow."

"Thanks," I say weakly as I stagger to my feet, Janine on the ground in tears only a few feet away.

And then, to Loder and Janine's utter astonishment, I straighten out, turn to Loder and say, "You know what? I'm suddenly feeling much better."

Proud of my Oscar-worthy performance, I uncork a pile-driver fist. The shocked Loder falls back, and I move in to crush another blow to his head. The blow sends Loder reeling back to where he had dropped his gun. He grabs for it and turns to fire just as I kick him hard in the middle, a move that pushes him into the vertical experimental chamber.

Loder quickly recovers and fires. Reflexively, I dive for cover, then spring back up and push the thick see-through plastic-composite door shut as Loder empties the clip, bullets pouring through the narrowing gap.

Once again, slugs penetrate the high-voltage equipment, causing shorts all over the place. Everything's crackling, lights are flickering, emergency sirens are wailing.

Activated by runaway signals, the panel just outside the chamber flashes to life. A panoply of overhead rays shoots down, bathing Loder in bright spectrums of blue energized light I recognize all too well from my time in a Genescence capsule. Only this must be a new and improved capsule, because the light is twice as intense, the sound twice as deafening. A readout on the panel flashes an alert in red: Warning: Maximum Radiation Exposure. Loder's eyes open wide as he's suddenly aware of his plight. He pounds on the glass wall, then smashes his way out and hurries off as I help Janine up.

"Don't worry," Janine says. "He won't get far."

Meanwhile, circuit breakers can't stop the onslaught. Fire is shooting out of dozens of electronic hot spots, and all of the generators and computers go out. Emergency backup lights come on, and the experimental chamber goes dark.

Then, like a long-awaited cavalry, Walter Greene and a contingent of FBI agents wearing assault gear burst in from every door and swarm across the entire facility. Walter rushes up and states the obvious: "Janine! You're hurt!"

He signals, and two of his men come over. Seeing Janine, they pull out first-aid equipment and stem the bleeding on her shoulder.

Walter turns to me, "What in God's name is going on?"

He's probably expecting the impetuous, sarcastic old Morgan to answer with some smart-ass comment. But the truth is, I'm grateful. Maybe it wasn't TimeLock that matured me. Maybe I had to get here on my own.

Much to Walter's surprise, I squeeze his shoulder and say, "The important thing is you got here just in time, Walter. Agent Greene. Thank you."

No less surprised at my uncharacteristically magnanimous behavior, a newly bandaged Janine smiles, then approaches a very confused Walter.

"I'm proud of you, Walter. You came."

"I had to find a judge to sign warrants. That was the sticky part. It was all . . ."

Janine smiles. "Highly irregular?"

Humorless as ever, Walter nods. "Exactly." Then, looking around, he once again states the obvious. "Say, we've got a major fire working here! Come on! Everybody out! Let's go!" Walter moves off, and I turn to Janine.

"Who's the most boring actor you can think of?"

"Why?"

"To play Walter in the movie."

She gives me a big smile as we join Walter and his team and start funneling toward the exit door. I look back to see Loder's dream and our nightmare turning to smoke and ashes.

CHAPTER THIRTY

By the time we arrive outside, the place is completely packed with media and guests. Marine One has just touched down on the Genescence helipad, and Secret Service agents flock to escort the president and Governor Myra Winters to an outdoor press area where reporters take their seats excitedly.

"Where's the welcoming committee?" an annoyed Governor Winters asks one of her terrified aides as Janine and I watch in bemusement from behind the curtain near the main stage. This is going to be great—front row seats as Myra Winters watches her precious TimeLock program quite literally go up in flames.

In the press area, the governor angrily approaches a Genescence media representative and says, "Where's Loder?"

The woman shrugs nervously and pulls out her cell phone. Just then, everyone murmurs as flames issue forth from the Genescence building. For the time being, the fire is fairly distant and seemingly innocuous, so nobody is overly alarmed except Governor Winters, who glares at the equally worried press woman and shouts, "What's going on here?"

The woman shrugs, and the governor moves behind the podium. A little fire, probably of zero consequence, she likely reasons, isn't going to dampen her historic presentation.

"Ladies and gentleman, my name is Governor Myra Winters, and I've been informed that a small fire broke out in the kitchen, but the only thing we have to worry about is a few overcooked prime ribs," she says amid nervous laughter.

"I'd like to welcome you to the headquarters of a truly revolutionary company you know all about called Genescence. We are here this evening to mark a historic milestone in the annals of American justice. And to share that milestone with you, please welcome a great leader and a true visionary, President William Bartlett!"

Amid a roar of applause, President Bartlett moves behind the podium, unable to even fake a smile as he passes Myra Winters.

"My fellow Americans," the president begins, "a page has been turned in America's war against crime. Tonight, I am here to announce the nationwide implementation of the most significant crime prevention program in this country's history—TimeLock. Effective tomorrow at nine o'clock in the morning, eastern time, TimeLock will be the law of the land in all fifty states of this great union. And, more than ever, I'm confident future generations will look back on this moment and say to themselves . . . WHAT THE FUCK WAS THAT?"

A huge explosion has just rocked the facility. The crowd breaks into frenzied panic, and then several people start to scream even louder as we all spot Patrick Loder running toward the president and Myra Winters.

And then we all realize what's happening. With every step, Loder's growing older and older. He's poor Charlie Rajek all over again, the time machine run amok. In a matter of seconds, he has passed 100 years old, and then, a few moments later, his entire body dissolves into a fine dust. A dust that floats through the air and lands right on Governor Myra Winters.

As the governor joins the chorus of screams, Secret Service agents surround her and the president and haul them off to the helicopter.

CHAPTER THIRTY-ONE

Transfixed by the flames, we watch fire engines arriving, quenching streams arcing against the orangey night sky as stunned employees look on. Huge explosions rock the area.

My arm is around Janine, and Walter glances over as though taking in, at last, our true relationship. Guess what? I actually feel bad for him. Of course, Janine was never going to settle down with a humorless man like Walter (I can imagine the vows: "Till boredom do you part . . ."), but he probably doesn't know that. And to lose her to some immature escaped felon like me, no less? That has to hurt, but being the practical, matter-of-fact person he is, I have a feeling he'll be just fine. I can't help but wonder when he will arrest me, though, because my time on the run has obviously just ended.

Fortunately, Walter moves off, and Dr. Garvey and Anna approach. We exchange warm greetings as we watch the inferno. Dr. Garvey puts a hand on my shoulder.

"I'm going back to the Fountain of Youth. Where it all began."

"I hope you find it this time," I say.

"Perhaps I will. Because I've learned a valuable lesson during this difficult ordeal, Morgan."

I look at him, once again awaiting profound words of wisdom from the sage elderly genius.

"Growing old sucks."

The man never stops surprising me. But the next thing he says tops it all by a mile.

"Especially the way you and I did it."

I'm more puzzled than ever. Then my eyes open wide: "My God! You went through TimeLock!"

"Five years ago. Strangely enough, I was the only volunteer for the first clinical trial. That, plus our friend Loder insisted."

"May I ask . . .?"

"How many years? Was supposed to only be three. But the kalopheen mix was all wrong, and I got thirty instead. Maybe we should start a club."

"Sign me up, Dr. Garvey."

"Actually, it's Dr. Garrett. Louis Garrett. And my wife's real name is Kiyoko. We met in Japan many years ago. I'll have to tell you the whole story someday."

"I'd like that," I respond sincerely. I smile briefly, but then a wave of sadness for the two of us sweeps over me.

Until the good doctor says, "Stay in touch, Morgan. There may be a way back for both of us."

He gives me a warm smile as his wife moves next to him. As much as I want to find out more, I decide to leave it be for the moment. If there is a "cure," somehow, someday, I know I'll see Dr. Garvey—or, more accurately, Dr. Garrett—again.

Janine moves toward me, and I again put my arm around her as the four of us collectively stare at the still-smoldering Genescence.

At long last, it looks like the horror that was TimeLock has ended. Which is great for the world, but of course doesn't let me off the hook. Not even close. In fact, Walter and a couple of agents are headed my way right now, and the message is clear: my days of freedom are over. Janine and I exchange resigned glances, and I'm promptly arrested and handcuffed.

CHAPTER THIRTY-TWO

THREE WEEKS LATER

Deep down, I knew this day would come. God knows Janine warned me countless times, but, somehow, I fantasized it would all miraculously end with complete exoneration and a get-out-of-jail-free card for life.

Alas, this is the real world, and it's time to face the music, even if the music in question turns out to be "Taps." Yes, given the damaging intel about Loder on the memory stick, I'm credited with helping expose TimeLock for what it was. Still, the harsh reality is that I'm still an escaped convict, and I may well be on my way back to Loomis to serve the second half of my forty-year sentence—this time the old-fashioned way over the next twenty years, since all TimeLock operations have been shut down pending a congressional inquiry.

Worse still, I'm sure to be found guilty for escaping and have a few more years added to my sentence. At this rate, I should get out in time for Janine's retirement party.

Speaking of Janine, she, of course, has gone to bat for me, submitting to DC-based Judge Monroe Gattick a sworn affidavit on my behalf in which she methodically and forthrightly lays out exactly what happened, with an obvious emphasis on Neil Colby's admission to us at Blue Lakes Resort that he, in fact, killed Lonny Myers. She also laid out my role in exposing Patrick Loder and Genescence, repeatedly risking my life to save others in the process.

Though I certainly didn't ask her to, Janine reluctantly fudged the truth a bit on one other crucial issue the judge will surely be considering. Rather than revealing that I did spend a few days on the run after breaking out of Loomis, Janine wrote that I offered to turn myself in right away (not really), and would have done so sooner had I not feared for my safety with Loder and his henchmen on my tail (maybe).

As you may recall, I did, in fact, offer to turn myself in a matter of days after my escape, but it wasn't a noble act of law-abiding self-sacrifice. It was a desperate gambit to team up with Janine and uncover what was going on with the TimeLock program.

The moment of truth has arrived, and I'm in the courtroom facing a very stern and humorless Judge Gattick. This isn't a jury trial like my first one. It's just me, my attorney, Janine, my mother, and a few others.

"I've read Agent Price's affidavit," the judge says, "and, while I found it compelling, I was forced to question its veracity based on her state of mind both then and now. More specifically, Mr. Eberly, not only was Agent Price put on leave from the FBI as a result of her interactions with you, but the two of you entered into a personal relationship that continues to this day. Is that not true?"

Janine and I exchange forlorn glances. This is going south fast. Before I can even answer, the judge continues: "In ordinary circumstances, I would add five years to your existing sentence and have you cuffed and taken back to Loomis posthaste."

Then the most unexpected thing in the world happens. Judge Gattick actually smiles. "But these aren't ordinary circumstances, are they Mr. Eberly?"

I start to answer, but am interrupted as the judge holds up two separate pieces of paper.

"Fortunately for you, Agent Price isn't the only one who has presented your side of the story for my consideration. Do you know what I have here?"

Again, I'm about to answer when the judge cuts me off. I may not get a word in all day, but I like where this is headed, so I'm more than happy to keep my mouth shut and my hopes up.

"This is a sworn affidavit from Walter Greene of the FBI not only corroborating much of what Agent Price wrote but adding a crucial new bit of information he discovered at her behest. Would you like to hear what he wrote, Mr. Eberly?"

No, I'd rather go polka dancing! Of *course* I want to hear it. Not bothering to speak this time, I nod enthusiastically.

"At the suggestion of Agent Price, the bureau further investigated the murder of Lawrence Myers, for which Mr. Eberly was originally convicted, and found two new pieces of exculpatory evidence. First among these is footage from a video surveillance camera located near a minimall on the road to Mr. Eberly's cabin showing a black sedan whose driver has been positively identified as Neil Colby. This footage was taken one hour before Mr. Eberly's arrival at his family's cabin and is completely in keeping with his subsequent testimony concerning both Neil Colby and the sedan.

"Secondly, upon further reflection, the witness who claimed to have seen Mr. Eberly force Mr. Myers into the cabin now recalls there having been two men at the scene and also remembers wondering who the black sedan belonged to. Furthermore, the witness did not see Mr. Eberly arrive, and says she definitely would have noticed someone riding a motorcycle, as opposed to driving a traditional vehicle.

"Given these new details," Judge Gattick continues, "coupled with Agent Price's testimony concerning Neil Colby's alleged confession to the murder, I am prepared to dismiss the original charge against Mr. Eberly and to apologize to him for the years lost to him because of this patently unfair conviction."

Janine and I exchange huge smiles, but the judge isn't through. In fact, his expression grows serious, and I realize I'm not off the hook yet. There's still the little matter of my escape.

"Mr. Eberly, while a grave injustice was done to you, it does not legally or morally excuse your violation of the law when you escaped from Loomis. As you must know, this act is a crime in and of itself, and I am duty bound to treat it as such regardless of your innocence on the original murder charge. Do you understand, Mr. Eberly?"

I nod.

"Good," the judge says. Then it happens again—he smiles! Holding up another piece of paper, he starts to read. "'In my humble opinion, our justice system and our nation as a whole owe Morgan Eberly a true debt of gratitude. Despite being stripped of twenty years of his life for a crime he didn't commit, he risked his life to help expose criminal acts that took place without my knowledge at Genescence. As a result of the bravery shown by him, Agent Price, Director Greene, and others, TimeLock has been contained, and the ruthless reign of Genescence CEO Patrick Loder has been neutralized. The decision, of course, is yours, but I urge you in the strongest possible terms to consider not only exonerating Morgan Eberly but thanking him for bringing our beloved country back from the brink. Yours Truly, Dr. Lionel Garvey.'"

My eyes instantly tear up, and Janine and my mom are no less moved. I'm sure Janine knew all about Walter's affidavit and didn't want to tell me in advance for fear of getting my hopes too high. But she's clearly as surprised and touched by Dr. Garvey's words as I am.

Five minutes later, the judge dismisses all charges, thanks me for all I've done, and brings the gavel down on my supposed life of crime forever.

CHAPTER THIRTY-THREE

THREE MONTHS LATER

Janine and I are in her condo. I practically live here now. Nothing—at least, nothing *yet*—can give me my missing twenty years back, but I've never been happier in my life. My mother is well, and she's crazy about Janine. I've started my own tech consulting business and have a half dozen clients already. Guess the gray temples give me an added air of credibility, so I do have that one thing to thank TimeLock for.

Most importantly, Janine and I are thriving. When all this started, there were times I guess we both wondered if this was more of a wartime romance than a true relationship. But that all changed along the way for both of us. I'm not sure exactly when for her, but for me it was the night at the River Inn. Not because we wound up in bed together, but because it was the first time I could seriously picture myself as a husband and even a father. Maybe seeing time fly by so quickly had finally jostled me out of my shallow youthful impetuousness and made me someone who not only was ready for a woman like Janine, but worthy of her as well.

Guess I have TimeLock to thank for that too.

Reinstated after the raid on Genescence (and fully recovered from her shoulder injury), Janine is once again Walter's favorite protégé and a hero within the agency as a whole for bringing down Loder and exposing TimeLock for the affront that it was. It's true that most of Janine's FBI colleagues had supported the program, but showing them what was really behind the curtain, of course, changed everything.

The TV is on, and our attention is drawn to Governor Myra Winters on cable news with anchor Gene Wheeler.

"What about TimeLock, Governor? Is it dead and buried?"

The governor has avoided talking about TimeLock since that fateful night at Genescence, and President

Bartlett, as evidenced by that open-mic tape from a couple of years back, was never all that sure about the program to begin with.

Given what we were able to prove about the late Patrick Loder (with Dr. Garvey fully absolved of any blame), we're not surprised that the governor has moved on. Yes, crime is back up, but we can't imagine she'd want to launch her likely presidential campaign reminding voters of her program's devastating failure.

Which is why Janine and I are stunned to hear her response to Wheeler's question: "In its previous incarnation, yes."

What does that mean? Wheeler is no less taken aback.

"That would seem to imply *re*incarnation. Is that what your meeting with the president was about last week?"

"No comment."

"Well, I don't have to tell you about the rumors flooding this town since your visit to the White House. A new program through a resurrected Genescence, maybe by next year? Just in time for your expected presidential candidacy."

This can't be happening!

"I think that's jumping the gun," Governor Winters replies with well-rehearsed circumspection. "But we do know there are many tough issues facing this country, Gene. And not only from within."

Janine and I exchange worried glances. Where is she going with this?

"What about Dr. Garvey's warnings not to resurrect the program? That it could happen again?"

"My own feeling is that TimeLock called for surveillance and oversight that was never properly imposed. Tight safeguards would have prevented the involvement of people like Loder and the hoodlums he brought in."

"Are you suggesting hands-on government supervision, like NASA or the Manhattan Project?"

"You're putting words in my mouth, Gene." Then a cryptic smile crosses the governor's face, and she adds, "But the Manhattan Project has come to mind."

"How about the fact that President Bartlett has repeatedly said TimeLock will never see the light of day again on his watch."

"That's true, but let's not forget that his watch stops ticking a year from January 20."

She produces a Mona Lisa smile, and the screen behind Wheeler is filled with familiar images of protests against

TimeLock. But this time, a few "pro" signs appear. Among the signs we can make out: "The 'Age' of TimeLock Is Over!" and "Stopping TimeLock Would Be a Crime!"

And this from Wheeler: "Our subject tonight: is there still a future for the TimeLock program? We'll invite our panel of experts to provide their analysis after this short break."

We mute the television and stare at it, both utterly incredulous.

"They're doing it. All over again. I don't believe it," Janine says.

"Believe it," I say. Then Janine reacts to my pensive look. "What's with the face?"

"Just thinking . . ."

"What?"

"Something's wrong."

"What could be wrong? You're a free man. You bought a new motorcycle. You finally learned how to shave. Life's good."

"Hit men? Attack helicopters? Even for a guy with Loder's resume, doesn't that all seem a little . . . *extravagant* . . . for a genetics company?"

"What are you saying? Someone else was pulling the strings all that time?"

"Maybe."

"Who did you have in mind?"

I gesture to the TV, on which Wheeler and a panel are deep in discussion. Behind them is a giant photo of Myra Winters.

Janine grows suddenly quiet.

"You think I'm crazy, right?" I ask.

"It's not that . . ."

"What then?"

"Nothing."

"Yeah, right," I say sarcastically. "I know your nothings, and this is something."

She continues to hesitate, then I add, "I thought we didn't keep secrets from each other."

"I'm an FBI agent, Morgan! Of *course* I keep secrets from you. And this one is beyond classified."

Sometimes silence is more persuasive than words, so I don't utter a syllable while Janine thinks it over for a long minute.

"Screw it," she finally says. "You of all people deserve to know. But not a word to anyone, Morgan. And that includes all of your deep-state friends on the internet."

"Deep web."

"Whatever. I mean it. If this leaks, I'm out on my ass for good this time."

"All right. I understand. What's going on?"

"I have it on good authority—"

"Walter."

"I didn't say that."

"Okay, let's just call him an unnamed source whom I've grown rather fond of despite the fact that he's as exciting as paint remover."

"Fine. Walter's family is quite close to the Bartletts. In fact, the president and Walter have been golfing buddies for years. And, according to Bartlett, the reason Myra Winters paid him a visit in the Oval last week was to broach an insane proposition having to do with TimeLock."

"I knew she wouldn't let it die."

"It's worse than that. She doesn't want to restart the program. She wants to reinvent it. You saw how she reacted just now to the words *Manhattan Project*."

"Wait a minute," I say rather loudly. "She wants to *weaponize* TimeLock! How exactly would that work?"

"By creating a modified version of the process in aerosol form. I think the idea is that it would cause rapid cellular degradation among enemy soldiers on the battlefield. Like Havana syndrome but a thousand times more powerful."

"Okay. Let me get this straight. Her brilliant idea is to turn enemy soldiers into the cast of *Cocoon?*"

"No. Nothing involving aging, and nothing as obvious as what you went through. Very subtle but very effective. A form of undetectable and easily transmissible cellular deconstruction that would wreak havoc on our opponents' reflexes and cognitive abilities."

"Please tell me Bartlett shut her down and kicked her out."

"According to Walter, he told her she was certifiable. That what she was proposing was not only illegal but immoral. But, apparently, she didn't care. She said it was the best way to win a war or maybe even prevent one in the first place."

"Janine, this woman is almost certainly going to be our next president. Can't Bartlett go public with this?"

"She'd just deny it. Claim that Bartlett has always had it in for her. And let's not forget that she's far more popular than he is. I mean, her pet program comes crashing down, yet she somehow emerges from the whole scandal unscathed?" Janine pauses for a moment, then says, "Morgan, I don't know if Myra Winters can be stopped."

"One way to find out."

"And what's that?"

"After she's elected, if she's elected, we team up again. Keep an eye on her every move. You through the bureau, me through—well, maybe it's better if you don't know what I'm up to." I give her a big smile and add, "I have a few secrets of my own, you know."

Janine shakes her head and smiles. She moves in close.

"My life was a lot simpler before you barreled your way into it."

I pat her stomach. "Just think—without me, you'd probably have decided to play it safe, marry your boring boss and become pregnant with Walter Junior."

"And without me, you'd probably have been sent back to Loomis, given the rest of your forty-year sentence, and been forced to live out your days as Morgan Senior."

I break into another big smile, then Janine says, "You want me to say it? Fine. I'm glad you burst into my life. You're a pain the ass, but I love you, and I hope you stay right here."

I catch the still-televised photo of Myra Winters in the corner of my eye and turn the TV off. I can't look at her face another second. But I have a feeling we're not done with her. Not by a long shot.

For now, though, the only woman I want to focus on is Janine. So I draw her closer and say this: "I love you too. And, just to be clear, I'm not going anywhere."

"Good," says Janine as she leans in to kiss me. "Because luckily for you, I like older men."

THE END

COMING SOON

TIMELOCK 2

Morgan and Janine rush to Japan to rescue Dr. Garvey, the geneticist who had been forced to create TimeLock and who is now being compelled by the deranged new U.S. President to create a weaponized version of TimeLock for use on the battlefield. After returning to America, Morgan is grabbed and taken to an ad hoc research facility in Siberia to undergo genetic experimentation along with dozens of other prisoners. The experience is nightmarish, but there's one glimmer of hope if he can escape–Dr. Garvey may be close to finding a way to reverse Morgan's 20-year TimeLock aging process once and for all.

ABOUT THE AUTHORS

An award-winning novelist and screen-writer, Howard Berk's credits include memorable episodes of such classic TV series as *Columbo, Mission: Impossible* and *The Rockford Files*, as well as the feature film, *Target*, starring Gene Hackman and Matt Dillon.

Peter Berk has written six novels, three TV pilots and a dozen screenplays, including several with his father which became the basis for the *TimeLock* series of novellas. Peter and his family live in Southern California.

IngramElliott Publishing

IngramElliott is an award-winning independent publisher with a mission to bring great stories to light in print and on-screen. We publish stories that will translate well into film, broadcast, and streaming television projects across many popular genres. We look for a great story, unique voice, and the author's ability to build a strong platform. Please review our current submission guidelines for more information.

IE Snaps!
by
IngramElliott

Our IE Snaps! imprint features novella-length genre fiction in favorite genres like action, thriller, mystery, romance, and young adult. These titles are designed for a quick read on the go. Visit our website for all of our IngramElliott and IE Snaps! titles and to follow us on social media.

www.ingramelliott.com

9 781952 961076